KU-634-611

'Surely I can do this,' Mia whispered. 'I've come so far since those days— surely I can do this?'

She closed her eyes, but nothing could stop those memories as she allowed herself the luxury of picturing Carlos O'Connor in her mind's eye. Luxury? Or was it a torment?

How could she forget the satanic edge to his looks that was so intriguing—irresistible, but at the same time capable of making you feel you were playing with fire?

Or not remember the way he laughed sometimes and that wicked sense of humour?

Or those times when no one would have suspected he was at the helm of a multinational construction company? Times when he'd exchanged his suits for jeans and a T-shirt and indulged his favourite pastimes: sailing, riding, flying. In fact he was rarely formal, when she thought about it.

But, above all, how could she ever forget lying in Carlos O'Connor's arms?

Lindsay Armstrong was born in South Africa, but now lives in Australia with her New Zealand-born husband and their five children. They have lived in nearly every state of Australia, and have tried their hand at some unusual—for them—occupations, such as farming and horse-training: all grist to the mill for a writer! Lindsay started writing romances when their youngest child began school and she was left feeling at a loose end. She is still doing it and loving it.

Recent titles by the same author:

WHEN ONLY DIAMONDS WILL DO
THE GIRL HE NEVER NOTICED
THE SOCIALITE AND THE CATTLE KING
ONE-NIGHT PREGNANCY

Did you know these are also available as eBooks?
Visit www.millsandboon.co.uk

THE RETURN OF HER PAST

BY
LINDSAY ARMSTRONG

All the characters in this book have no existence outside the imagination of the author, and have no relation whatsoever to anyone bearing the same name or names. They are not even distantly inspired by any individual known or unknown to the author, and all the incidents are pure invention.

All Rights Reserved including the right of reproduction in whole or in part in any form. This edition is published by arrangement with Harlequin Enterprises II BV/S.à.r.l. The text of this publication or any part thereof may not be reproduced or transmitted in any form or by any means, electronic or mechanical, including photocopying, recording, storage in an information retrieval system, or otherwise, without the written permission of the publisher.

® and TM are trademarks owned and used by the trademark owner and/or its licensee. Trademarks marked with ® are registered with the United Kingdom Patent Office and/or the Office for Harmonisation in the Internal Market and in other countries.

First published in Great Britain 2013
by Mills & Boon, an imprint of Harlequin (UK) Limited.
Harlequin (UK) Limited, Eton House, 18-24 Paradise Road,
Richmond, Surrey TW9 1SR

© Lindsay Armstrong 2013

ISBN: 978 0 263 23502 9

Harlequin (UK) policy is to use papers that are natural, renewable and recyclable products and made from wood grown in sustainable forests. The logging and manufacturing process conform to the legal environmental regulations of the country of origin.

MORAY COUNCIL LIBRARIES & INFO.SERVICES	
20 35 80 75	
Askews & Holts	
RF RF	

THE RETURN
OF HER PAST

PROLOGUE

MIA GARDINER WAS home alone and preparing dinner for her mother when the storm hit with very little warning.

One minute she was rolling pastry, the next she was racing around the big old house known as West Windward and home to the wealthy O'Connor family, closing windows and doors as raindrops hammered down on the roof like bullets.

It was when she came to close the front door that a dark, damp figure loomed through the outside gloom and staggered towards her.

For a moment her heart leapt into her throat in fright, then she recognised the figure.

'Carlos! It's you. What are you doing—Carlos, are you all right?' She stared up at him, taking in the fact that he had blood pouring down his temple from a nasty-looking cut. 'What happened?' she breathed and clutched him as he swayed where he stood.

'A branch came down as I was crossing from the garage to the house. Hit me on the head,' he said indistinctly. 'That's quite a storm,' he added.

'You're not wrong.' Mia put her hand on his arm. 'Come with me. I'll fix your head.'

'What I need is a strong drink!' But he swayed again as he said it.

'Come,' she said, and led him through the house to the housekeeper's sitting room. It opened off the kitchen and was small but comfortable.

Mia cleared her mother's knitting off the settee and Carlos O'Connor collapsed gratefully onto it. In fact he lay down and groaned and closed his eyes.

Mia was galvanised into action. Half an hour later she had cleaned and dressed the cut on his head whilst not only rain but hail teemed down outside.

Then the lights went off and she clicked her tongue, mainly because she should have expected it. They had frequent power failures in the district when the weather was stormy. Fortunately her mother kept some kerosene lamps handy but in the dark she tripped around until she located them. Then she lit a couple and brought one into the sitting room.

Carlos was lying unmoving, his eyes were closed and he looked very pale.

She stared down at him and felt a wave of tenderness flow through her because the truth of the matter was that Carlos O'Connor was gorgeous. All the lean six foot plus length of him, the dark hair, testament to his Spanish heritage, that he often pushed out of his eyes, those grey eyes that sometimes glinted wickedly at you...

She'd had a crush on Carlos since she was fifteen— how could you not? she sometimes wondered. How could anyone be immune to that devastatingly sexy aura? He might be ten years older than her eighteen years but surely she could catch up?

Not that she'd seen an awful lot of him over the past five years. He didn't live on the property but she believed he'd grown up on it; he lived in Sydney, but he did come back from time to time. Usually it was only for a couple of days but he rode, not only horses but quad bikes, and because Mia was allowed to stable her horse on the property, and because she kept a weather eye on his horses when she was home, they had a bit in common.

She'd had some marvellous gallops with Carlos and if he'd ever divined that sometimes he made her heart-beat triple he'd never given any sign of it.

At first her daydreams had been simple and girlish but over the last couple of years she'd graduated from alternating between telling herself to forget all about Carlos O'Connor—he was a multi-millionaire, she was only the housekeeper's daughter—and some rather more sophisticated daydreams.

Still, he was way out of her league. What could she offer him over the gorgeous beauties who sometimes accompanied him on his visits?

'Mia?'

She came out of her daydream with a start and saw that his eyes were open.

'How do you feel?' She knelt down beside him and put the lamp down. 'Do you have a headache? Or double vision? Or any strange symptoms?'

'Yes.' He thought for a moment.

She waited, then, 'What? Tell me. I don't think I can get a doctor to come out in this—' she gestured up towards the cacophony on the roof above '—but—'

'I don't need a doctor,' he murmured and reached for her. 'Just this. You've grown up, Mia, grown up and grown gorgeous...'

Mia gasped as his arms closed about her and somehow, she wasn't sure how, she ended up lying beside him on the settee. 'Carlos!' she remonstrated and tried to sit up. 'What are you doing?'

'Relax,' he murmured.

'But—well, apart from anything else, you could have a fractured skull!'

'If I did, quiet and warmth and comfort would be recommended, don't you agree?' he suggested gravely.

'I...you...perhaps but—' Mia broke off helplessly.

'That's exactly what you could provide, Miss Gardiner. So would you mind not wriggling around like a trapped pilchard?'

'A trapped pilchard?' Mia repeated in outraged tones. 'How dare you, Carlos?'

'Sorry. Not the most complimentary analogy. How about a trapped siren? Yes, that's better, don't you agree?' And he ran his hands down her body, then cuddled her against him. 'Pilchard. I must be crazy!' he murmured.

Mia took a breath to tell him he was crazy but suddenly she was laughing. Then they were laughing together and it was the most wonderful thing that had ever happened to Mia.

So much so, she lay quietly in his arms and when he

started to kiss her, she didn't resist. She was powerless to be unaffected by the amazing rapture he brought to her as he kissed her and held her. As he told her she had the most luscious mouth, skin like silk and hair like midnight.

She was made conscious of her body in ways she'd never known before as delicious ripples of desire ran through her. She was deeply appreciative of his easy strength and his long clean lines, the width of his shoulders and the way his hands brought her so much pleasure.

In fact she started to kiss him back and, when it was over, once again she lay quietly against him, her arms around him and she was deeply affected by everything about him. Not only that but conscious that it wasn't impossible for him to be attracted to an eighteen-year-old—why else would he be doing this? Why else would he tell her she'd grown up and grown gorgeous?

Surely it couldn't be concussion?

Two days later Mia drove away from the O'Connor estate and set her course, so to speak, for Queensland, where she'd been offered a university place.

She'd said goodbye to her parents, who'd been proud but just a little sad, but she was secure in the knowledge that they loved their jobs. Her father had a great deal of respect for Frank O'Connor, who'd built his construction company into a multi-million dollar business, although he'd recently suffered a stroke and been confined to a wheelchair, leaving his son Carlos in charge.

It was Carlos's mother Arancha, a diminutive Spanish lady, a beauty in her earlier days but still the epitome of style, who had given her only son a Spanish name and it was she amongst the O'Connors who loved the Hunter Valley estate of West Windward passionately.

But it was Mia's mother who actually tended the homestead, with all its objets d'art, priceless carpets and exquisite linens and silks. And it was her father who looked after the extensive gardens.

To some extent Mia shared both her parents' talents. She loved to garden and the greatest compliment her father had given her was to tell her she had 'green fingers'. She also took after her mother in her eye for decorative detail and love of fine food.

Mia was conscious that she owed her parents a lot. They'd scrimped and saved to give her the best education at a private boarding school. That was why she always helped as much as she could when she was home with them and she knew she was fulfilling their dream by going to university.

But as she drove away two days after the storm, her thoughts were in chaos, her head was still spinning and she didn't look back.

CHAPTER ONE

'CARLOS O'CONNOR WILL be attending,' Mia Gardiner's assistant Gail announced in hushed, awed tones.

Mia's busy hands stilled for a moment—she was arranging a floral display. Then she carried on placing long-stemmed roses in a standard vase. 'He is the bride's brother,' she said casually.

Gail lowered the guest list and stared at her boss. 'How do you know that? They don't have the same surname.'

'Half-brother, actually,' Mia corrected herself. 'Same Spanish mother, different fathers. She's a couple of years older. I think she was about two when her father died and her mother remarried and had Carlos.'

'How do you know *that*?' Gail demanded.

Mia stood back, admired her handiwork but grimaced inwardly. 'Uh—there's not a lot that isn't known about the O'Connors, I would have thought.'

Gail pursed her lips but didn't disagree and studied the guest list instead. 'It says—it just says Carlos O'Connor and partner. It doesn't say who the partner is. I thought I read something about him and Nina

French.' Gail paused and shrugged. 'She's gorgeous. And wouldn't it be lovely to have all that money? I mean he's got a fortune, hasn't he? And he's gorgeous too, Carlos O'Connor. Don't you think so?'

'Undoubtedly,' Mia replied and frowned down at the tub of pink and blue hydrangeas at her feet. 'Now, what am I going to put these in? I know, the Wedgwood soup tureen—it sounds odd but they look good in it. How are *you* going, Gail?' she asked rather pointedly.

Gail awoke from her obviously pleasurable day-dream about Carlos O'Connor and sighed. 'I'm just about to lay the tables, Mia,' she said loftily and wafted away, pushing a cutlery trolley.

Mia grimaced and went to find the Wedgwood tureen.

Several hours later, the sun went down on Mount Wilson but Mia was still working. Not arranging flowers; she was in the little office that was the headquarters of the Bellbird Estate.

It was from this office in the grand old homestead, the main house on the estate, that she ran the reception function business, Bellbird Estate, a business that was becoming increasingly well-known.

Not only did the old house lend its presence to functions but its contents delighted Mia. It contained lovely pieces of old furniture, vases, lamps, linen and a beautiful china collection—including the Wedgwood tureen.

She catered for wedding receptions, iconic birthday parties—any kind of reception. The cuisine she provided was superb, the house and the gardens were lovely but perhaps the star of the show was Mount Wilson itself.

At the northern end of the Blue Mountains, west of Sydney, it had been surveyed in 1868 and had gradually acquired a similar reputation to an Indian 'hill station'—English-style homes with cool-climate English gardens in alien settings, this setting being bush and rainforest.

And anyone's first impression of Mount Wilson had to be how beautiful it was. Yes, the road was narrow and clung to the mountainside in tortuous zigzags in places but the trees in the village—plane trees, limes, elms, beeches and liquid ambers, were, especially when starting to wear their autumnal colours, glorious. There were also native eucalypts, straight, strong and reaching for the sky, and native tree ferns everywhere.

The glimpses of houses through impressive gateways and beyond sweeping driveways were tantalising, many old and stone with chimneys, some smothered in creepers like wisteria, others with magnificent gardens.

All in all, she'd thought often although she kept it to herself, Mount Wilson shouted money—new money or old money but *money*—and the resources to have acres of garden that you opened to the public occasionally. The resources to have an estate in the Blue Mountains, a retreat from the hurly-burly of Sydney or the heat of its summers....

And tomorrow Juanita Lombard, Carlos O'Connor's half-sister, was marrying Damien Miller on Mount Wilson—at Bellbird, to be precise. Damien Miller, whose mother, rather than the bride or her mother, had booked the venue without mentioning who the bride was until it was too late for Mia to pull out without damaging her business reputation.

Mia got up, stretched and rubbed her back and decided enough was enough; she'd call it a day.

She didn't live in the main house; she lived in the gardener's cottage, which was in fact a lot more modern, though unusual. It had been built as an artist's studio. The walls were rough brick, the plentiful woodwork was native timber and the floors were sandstone cobbles. It had a combustion stove for heating, a cook's delight kitchen and a sleeping loft accessible by ladder.

It was an interior that lent itself well to Mia's photography hobby, her images of native wildlife and restful landscapes, enlarged and framed, graced the walls. It also suited her South American poncho draped over a rail, her terracotta tubs full of plants and her chunky crockery.

It was also not far from the stables and that was where she went first, to bring her horse, Long John Silver, in from the paddock, to rug him and feed him.

Although it was summer, there were patches of mist clinging to the tree tops and the air was chilly enough to nip at your fingers and cheeks and turn the end of your nose pink. But the sunset was magical, a streaky symphony of pink and gold and she paused for a long moment with her arms around Long John's neck to wonder at life. Who would have thought Carlos O'Connor would cross her path again?

She shook her head and led Long John into his stall. She mixed his feed and poured it into his wall bin, checked his water, then, with a friendly pat and a flick of his mane through her fingers, she closed him in.

That was when she came to grief. She'd collected some wood for her stove and was taking a last look at the sunset when, seemingly from nowhere, what she'd kept at bay for hours enveloped her—the memories she'd refused to allow to surface ever since she'd known who would be at tomorrow's wedding flooded back to haunt her.

'Surely I can do this,' she whispered. 'I've come so far since those days—surely I can do this?'

She closed her eyes but nothing could stop those memories as she allowed herself the luxury of picturing Carlos O'Connor in her mind's eye. Luxury? Or was it a torment?

Whatever, how could she forget that night-dark hair that sometimes fell in his eyes? That olive skin his Spanish mother had bequeathed, yet the grey eyes that came from his Irish father and could be as cool as the North Sea or so penetrating his glance made you mentally sit up in a flurry and hope like mad you had your wits about you.

How could she forget the satanic edge to his looks that was so intriguing; irresistible but at the same time capable of making you feel you were playing with fire?

Or not remember the way he laughed sometimes and that wicked sense of humour?

Or the times when no one would have suspected he was at the helm of a multi-national construction company. Times when he exchanged his suit for jeans and T-shirt and indulged his favourite pastimes—sailing, riding, flying. In fact he was rarely formal when she thought about it. But above all how could she ever forget lying in Carlos O'Connor's arms?

She stood perfectly still for a long moment, then she reached into her pocket for a tissue and mopped herself up, determined that she would recover her equilibrium before tomorrow.

Mercifully, when she woke early the next morning, it was to see that at least the weather was fine; the sun had just started to climb into a cloudless sky. She had all sorts of contingency plans for wet weather but it was a relief not to have to resort to them.

She got up, dressed swiftly in jeans and an old shirt and brewed herself a cup of tea, which she took out into the garden. She loved the garden, all five acres of it, and although Bellbird employed a gardener it was Mia who supervised what went in and came out, something that led her into frequent discord with the gardener, Bill James, a man in his sixties who'd lived all his life on the mountain. Bill and his wife, Lucy, lived in another cottage on the property.

Lucy James was away at the moment. She made an annual pilgrimage to spend a month with her daughter and her six grandchildren in Cairns. To Mia's regret, Bill drove Lucy up to and back from Cairns but only ever stayed a couple of days with them.

That left Mia in the position of having to cope with Bill living on his own and hating it until Lucy returned. If he was cranky when his wife was present, he was ten times crankier when she wasn't.

Still, it had been a huge stroke of luck how she'd come to be able to start her reception business at Bellbird in the first place. She'd met the two old ladies, sisters and spinsters and now in their late eighties, who owned Bellbird, at Echo Point.

It had been her first visit to the Blue Mountains' premier tourist attraction, from which you could look over the Three Sisters and the Jamison Valley.

From the viewing platform she'd gazed out over the scenery and been enchanted by the wondrous views.

The elderly sisters had sat down on the bench beside her and struck up a conversation. Before long she'd learnt about the estate on Mount Wilson, the fact that the sisters now lived in a retirement home in Katoomba, which they hardly had a good word to say for. And the fact that they were looking for a use for their estate.

Mia had explained that she'd come up to the Blue Mountains with the idea of opening a function business—and things had progressed from there. Of course the sisters had had her vetted but what had started out as a business venture had blossomed into a friendship and Mia often visited them in their despised retirement home that was actually very luxurious and well-run. And she often took them bunches of flowers and snippets of gossip about the mountain because she could well imagine what it must be like living away from Bellbird.

If there was one area of concern for her regarding the estate it was that her lease was renewed annually and due for renewal shortly. Her two spinsters would be perfectly happy to renew it but had let drop that they

were under some pressure from their nephew, their clos-
est relative and heir, to think of selling Bellbird and in-
vesting the money for a higher return than the estate
was earning them.

On the morning of the Lombard/Miller wedding, things
at Mount Wilson were looking pretty grand. The gardens were in spectacular form and so was the house,
Mia noted, as she reluctantly went indoors and did a
thorough inspection.

The ceremony was to be conducted by a marriage
celebrant in an elegant rotunda in the garden, whilst the
meal was to be served in the huge main dining room
that easily seated the estimated seventy-five guests. It
was a spectacular room with a pressed iron ceiling and
long glass doors that opened onto the terrace and the
main rose garden.

Dancing would be in the atrium with its cool tiled
floor, and tables and chairs were dotted around the
main lawn.

'Well, it all looks good,' Mia said to the newly arrived Gail—she lived on the mountain only a few minutes' drive away. 'And here come the caterers. OK!
Let's get started.' And she and Gail gave each other a
high five salute as was their custom.

In the time she had before the wedding party arrived
Mia took a last look into the wedding suite—where the
members of the bridal party would dress and be able to
retire to if need be. And, content that it was all spick

and span, she jogged to her own quarters, where she took a shower and dressed herself for the event.

She studied herself thoughtfully in the mirror when she was ready. She always contrived to look elegant enough to be a guest but a discreet one, and today she was wearing a slim short-sleeved jade-green Thai silk dress with fashionable but medium heels in matching leather and a string of glass beads on a gold chain. She also wore a hat, more of a fascinator, to be precise. A little cap made from the same Thai silk with feathers and a froth of dotted voile worn on the side of her head.

He probably won't recognise me, she reassured herself as she stood in front of her cheval mirror admiring her reflection, and particularly the lovely fascinator, which seemed to invest her with more sophistication than she usually exhibited.

But even without the hat she was a far cry from the kind of girl she'd been in those days. Always in jeans, always outdoors, always riding when she could get away with it. Her clothes—her hair alone must look different from how she used to wear it. She grimaced.

Her hair was a sore point with her. Nearly black, it was wild and curly, yet it never looked right when it was cut to be manageable. So she wore it severely tied back when she was being formal, something she'd not done when she was younger.

Nothing, she had to acknowledge, had changed about her eyes, though. They were green and Gail had once told her her eyelashes were utterly to die for and so was her mouth. She also possessed a pair of dimples that she wasn't a hundred per cent keen on—they didn't seem to go with the sophisticated woman of the world she liked to hope she resembled.

She turned away from the mirror with a shrug and discovered, to her horror, that she was trembling finely because she was scared to death all of a sudden.

No, not all of a sudden, she corrected herself. Ever since she'd realised who the bride was, she'd been pretending to herself that she was quite capable of dealing with the O'Connor family when, underneath that, she'd been filled with the desire to run, to put as much distance between them as she could.

Now it was too late. She was going to have to go through with it. She was going to have to be civil to Arancha O'Connor and her daughter Juanita. Somehow she was going to have to be normal with Carlos.

Unless they didn't recognise her.

She took a deep breath and put her shoulders back; she could do it.

But all her uncertainties resurfaced not much later when she moved the Wedgwood tureen with its lovely bounty of hydrangeas to what she thought was a better spot—her last act of preparation for the Lombard/Miller wedding—and she dropped it.

It smashed on the tiled floor, soaking her feet in the process. She stared down at the mess helplessly.

'Mia?' Gail, alerted by the crash, ran up and surveyed the mess.

'I'm s-sorry,' Mia stammered, her hand to her mouth. 'Why did I do that? It was such a lovely tureen too.'

Gail looked up and frowned at her boss. At the same time it dawned on her that Mia had been different over the last few days, somehow less sure of herself, but why, she had no idea. 'Just an accident?' she suggested.

'Yes. Of course,' Mia agreed gratefully but still, apparently, rooted to the spot.

'Look, you go and change your shoes,' Gail recommended, 'and I'll clean up the mess. We haven't got much time.'

'Thank you! Maybe we could get it fixed?'

'Maybe,' Gail agreed. 'Off you go!'

Mia finally moved away and didn't see the strange look her assistant bestowed on her before she went to get the means to sweep up what was left of the Wedgwood tureen.

The wedding party arrived on time.

Mia watched through the French windows and saw the bride, the bridesmaids and the mother of the bride arrive. And for a moment she clutched the curtain with one hand and her knuckles were white, her face rigid as she watched the party, particularly the bride's mother, Arancha O'Connor. She took a deep breath, counted to ten and went out to greet them.

It was a hive of activity in the bridal suite. Mia provided a hairdresser, a make-up artist and a florist and in this flurry of dryers and hairspray, perfumes both bottled and from the bouquets and corsages, with the swish of petticoats and long dresses, laces and satins, it seemed safe to Mia to say that no one recognised her.

She was wrong.

The bridal party was almost ready when Arancha

O'Connor, the epitome of chic in lavender with a huge
hat, suddenly pointed at Mia and said, 'I know who you
are! Mia Gardiner.'

Mia turned to her after a frozen moment. 'Yes, Mrs
O'Connor. I didn't think you'd remember me.'

'Of course I remember you! My, my, Mia—' Arancha's dark gaze swept over her comprehensively
'—you've certainly acquired a bit of polish. Come up a
bit in the world, have we? Although—' Arancha looked
around '—I suppose this is just an upmarket version
of a housekeeping position, really! Juanita, do you remember Mia?' She turned to her daughter. 'Her parents
worked for us. Her mother in the kitchen, her father in
the gardens.'

Juanita looked absolutely splendid in white lace and
tulle but she frowned a little distractedly. 'Hi, Mia. I
do remember you now but I don't think we really knew
each other; I was probably before your time,' she said.
'Mum—' she looked down at the phone in her hand
'—Carlos is running late and he'll be coming on his
own.'

Arancha stiffened. 'Why?'

'No idea.' Juanita turned to Mia. 'Would you be able
to rearrange the bridal table so there's not an embar-
rassingly empty seat beside Carlos?'

'Of course,' Mia murmured and went to move away
but Arancha put a hand on her arm.

'Carlos,' she confided, 'has a beautiful partner.
She's a model but also the daughter of an ambassador. Nina—'

'Nina French,' Mia broke in dryly. 'Yes, I've heard of her, Mrs O'Connor.'

'Well, unfortunately something must have come up for Nina not to be able to make it, but—'

'Carlos is quite safe from me, Mrs O'Connor, even without Ms French to protect him,' Mia said wearily this time. 'Quite safe, believe me. And now, if you'll excuse me, I'll get back to work.' She turned away but not before she saw the glint of anger in Arancha's dark eyes.

'It's going quite well,' Gail whispered some time later as she and Mia happened to pass each other.

Mia nodded but frowned. Only 'quite well'? What was wrong? The truth was she was still trembling with suppressed anger after her encounter with Arancha O'Connor. And it was impossible to wrest her mind from it.

Her skill at blending the right music, her talent for drawing together a group of people, her adroit handling of guests had deserted her because Arancha had reduced her from seasoned professional to merely the housekeeper's daughter.

'But *he's* not here!' Gail added.

'He's running late, that's all.'

Gail tut-tutted and went on her way, leaving Mia in her post of discreet observer but feeling helpless and very conscious that she was losing her grip on this wedding. Not only that but she was possessed of a boiling sense of injustice.

She'd actually believed she could show Arancha that she'd achieved a minor miracle. That she'd begun and prospered a business that had the rich and famous flocking to her door. Moreover she could hold her own amongst them; her clothes bore designer labels, her taste in food and décor and the special little things she brought to each reception was being talked about with admiration.

But what had she proved? Nothing. With a few well chosen words Arancha had demolished her achievements and resurrected her inferiority complex so that it seemed to her she was once more sitting on the sidelines, looking in. She was no closer to entering Arancha and Juanita's circle than she'd ever been. Not to mention Carlos's...

She'd believed she could no longer be accused of being the housekeeper's daughter as if it were an invisible brand she was doomed to wear for ever, but, if anything, it had got worse.

From a dedicated cook, a person to whom the smooth running of the household—the scent of fresh clean linen, the perfume of flowers, the magic of herbs not only for cooking but infusions as well—from that dedicated person to whom all those things mattered, her mother had been downgraded to a 'kitchen' worker.

Her father, her delightfully vague father who cared passionately about not only what he grew but the birds and the bees and anything to do with gardens, had suffered a similar fate.

She shook her head, then clamped her teeth onto her bottom lip and forced herself to get a grip.

That was when the snarl of a powerful motor made itself heard, not to the guests but to Mia, whose hearing was attuned to most things that came and went from Bellbird, and she slipped outside.

The motor belonged to a sports car, a metallic yellow two-door coupé. The car pulled up to a stone-spitting halt on the gravel drive and a tall figure in jeans jumped out, reached in for a bag, then strode towards her.

'I'm late, I know,' he said. 'Who are you?'

'I...I'm running the show,' Mia replied a little uncertainly.

'Good, you can show me where to change. I'm Carlos O'Connor, by the way, and I'm in deep trouble. I'm sure I've missed the actual ceremony but please tell me I haven't missed the speeches!' he implored. 'They'll never talk to me again.' He took Mia's elbow and led her at a fast pace towards the house.

'No, not the speeches,' Mia said breathlessly, 'and now you're here I can delay them a little longer while you change. In here!' She gestured to a doorway on the veranda that led directly to the bridal suite.

Carlos turned away from her. 'Would you let them know I'm here?'

'Sure.'

'*Muchas gracias.*' He disappeared through the doorway.

Mia stared at the door with her lips parted and her eyes stunned. He hadn't recognised her!

Which was what she'd hoped for but the awful irony was she hated the thought of it because it had to be that she'd meant so little to him she must have been almost instantly forgettable...

She swallowed, then realised with a start that she

still had a wedding to run and a message to deliver. She straightened her hat and entered the dining room and discreetly approached the bridal table, where she bent down to tell the bride and the groom that Mr O'Connor had arrived and would be with them as soon as he'd changed.

'Thank heavens!' Juanita said fervently and her brand new husband Damien agreed with her.

'I know I didn't need anyone to give me away,' Juanita continued, 'but I do need Carlos to make the kind of speech only he can make. Not only—' she put a hand on Damien's arm and glinted him a wicked little look '—to extol all my virtues but to liven things up a bit!'

Mia flinched.

'Besides which, Mum is starting to have kittens,' Juanita added. 'She was sure he'd had an accident.'

'I'd have thought your mother would have stopped worrying about Carlos years ago,' Damien remarked.

This time Juanita cast him a speaking look. 'Never,' she declared. 'Nor will she ever rest until she's found him a suitable wife.'

Mia melted away at this point and she hovered outside the bridal suite to be able to direct the latecomer to the dining room through the maze of passages.

She would have much preferred to delegate this to Gail, not to mention really making Gail's day, no doubt, but she was not to be seen.

After about five minutes when Carlos O'Connor still had not appeared, she glanced at her watch with a frown and knocked softly on the door.

It was pulled open immediately and Carlos was

dressed in his morning suit and all present and correct—apart from his hair, which looked as if he'd been
dragging fingers through it, and his bow tie, which he
had in his hand.

'I can't tie the blasted thing,' he said through his
teeth. 'I never could. Tell you what, if I ever get married I will bar all monkey suits and bow ties. Here!' He
handed Mia the tie. 'If you're in charge of the show,
you do it.'

Typically Carlos at his most arrogant, Mia thought,
because she was still hurt to the quick.

She took the tie from him with a swift upward glance
that was about as cold as she was capable of and stood
up on her toes to briskly and efficiently tie the bow tie.

'There.' She patted it briefly. 'Now, *if* you wouldn't
mind and seeing as you're already late as it is, this wedding awaits you.'

'Wait a moment.' A frown grew in Carlos's grey eyes
as he put his hands on her hips—an entirely inappropriate gesture between guest and wedding reception
manager—and he said incredulously, 'Mia?'

She froze, then forced herself to respond, 'Yes. Hi,
Carlos!' she said casually. 'I didn't think you'd recognised me. Uh…Juanita really needs you so…' She went
to turn away but he detained her.

'What are you mad about, Mia?'

She had to bite her lip to stop herself from blurting
out the truth, the whole truth and nothing but the truth.
Chapter and verse, in other words, of every reason she
had for…well, being as mad as she could ever recall.

She swallowed several times. 'I'm having a little

trouble getting this wedding going,' she said carefully at last. 'That's all. So—' She tried to pull away.

He slipped his hands up to her waist and said authoritatively, 'Hang on. It must be—six—seven years— since you ran away, Mia.'

'I didn't…I…well, I suppose I did,' she corrected herself. 'And yes, about that. But look, Carlos, this wedding is really dragging its feet and it's going to be my reputation on the line if I don't get it going, so would you please come and make the kind of speech only you can make, apparently, to liven things up?'

'In a moment,' he drawled. 'Wow!' His lips twisted as he stood her away from him and admired her from her toes to the tip of her fascinator and all the curves in between. Not only that but he admired her legs, the slenderness of her waist, the smoothness of her skin, her sweeping lashes and delectable mouth. 'Pardon my boyish enthusiasm, but this time you've really grown up, Mia.'

She bit her lip. Dealing with Carlos could be difficult at the best of times but she well recognised him in this mood—there would be no moving him until he was ready to be moved.

She heaved an inward sigh and mentally gritted her teeth. All right, two could play this game…

'You're looking pretty fine yourself, Mr O'Connor,' she said lightly. 'Although I must say I'm surprised your mother hasn't found a wife for you yet.'

'The last person I would get to choose a wife for me is my mother,' he said dryly. 'What brought that up?'

Mia widened her eyes not entirely disingenuously but

in surprise as well. And found she had to think quickly. 'Probably the venue and what's going on here,' she said with an ironic little glint. 'Mind you, things are about to flop here if I don't pull something out of the hat!' And she pulled away, successfully.

He stared at her for a long moment, then he started to laugh and Mia felt her heart pound because she'd gone for so long without Carlos, without his laugh, without his arms around her...

'I don't know what you expect me to do,' he said wryly.

'I don't care what you do, but if you don't come and do *something*, Carlos,' she threatened through her teeth, suddenly furious although she had no idea if it was with him or with herself, or the situation, 'I'll scream blue murder!'

CHAPTER TWO

'FEELING BETTER?'

Mia took another sip of brandy and looked around. Everyone had gone. The bridal party, the guests, the caterers, they'd all gone. The presents had all been loaded carefully into a station wagon and driven away.

Gail had gone home in seventh heaven because she'd not only seen Carlos, she'd spoken to him. And the wedding had been a success. It had livened up miraculously as soon as Carlos had made his speech and Juanita had thrown her arms around Mia and Gail and thanked them profusely for their contribution to her special day as she'd left.

Carlos had driven away in his metallic yellow car and Mia had kicked off her shoes and changed her Thai silk dress for a smock but, rather than doing any work, she'd sunk into an armchair in the foyer. Her hat sat on a chair beside her. She was perfectly dry-eyed but she felt as if she'd been run over by a bus.

It was quite normal to feel a bit flattened after a function—she put so much into each and every one of them—but this was different; this was an emotional flat liner of epic proportions. This was all to do with Carlos and the fact that she'd been kidding herself for years if she'd thought she'd gotten over him.

All to do with the fact that the feel of his hands on her hips and waist had awoken sensations throughout her body that had thrilled her, the fact that to think he hadn't recognised her had been like a knife through her heart.

That was when someone said her name and she looked up and moved convulsively to see him standing there only a foot or so away.

'But...but,' she stammered, 'you left. I saw you drive off.'

'I came back. I'm staying with friends just down the road. And you need a drink. Point me in the right direction.'

Mia hesitated, then gestured. He came back a few minutes later with a drinks trolley, poured a couple of brandies and now he was sitting opposite her in an armchair. He'd changed into khaki cargo trousers and a grey sweatshirt.

'Feeling better?' he asked again.

She nodded. 'Thanks.'

He frowned. 'Are you sure you're in the right job if it takes so much out of you, Mia?'

'It doesn't usually—' She stopped and bit her lip.

'Doesn't usually affect you like this?' he hazarded.

She looked down and pleated the material of her smock. 'Well, no.'

'So what was different about this one?'

'I don't know.' Mia shrugged. 'I suppose I didn't think any of you would recognise me.'

'Why the hell wouldn't we?' he countered.

She shrugged. 'I've changed.'

'Not that much.'

She bridled and looked daggers at him before swiftly veiling her eyes. 'That's what your mother tried to tell me. I'm just a souped-up version of the housekeeper's daughter, in other words.'

'I didn't say that,' he retorted. 'Since when did you get so thin-skinned, Mia?'

She took a very deep breath. 'I'm not,' she said stiffly.

'I can't work out whether you want us to think you have changed or not.'

'Don't worry about it, Carlos,' she advised coolly. 'In fact, thank you for getting me a drink but I'd be happy if you went back to your friends. I have a lot to do still.'

'Short of throwing me out,' he replied casually, 'which I doubt you could do, you're going to have to put up with me, Mia, until I'm ready to go. So, why don't you fill me in on the missing years? I'm talking about the years between the time you kissed me with considerable ardour then waltzed off to uni, and now.' His grey gaze rested on her sardonically.

Mia went white.

'I'm waiting,' he remarked.

She said something supremely uncomplimentary beneath her breath but she knew from the autocratic set of his jaw that he wouldn't let up until he got the answers he wanted.

'All right!' She said it through her teeth but he intervened.

'Hang on a moment.' He reached over and took her glass. 'Let's have another one.'

With the deepest reluctance, she told him about the intervening years. How her mother and father had retired and were living in the Northern Rivers district of New South Wales. How they'd started a small tea shop in a country town that was becoming well known, not only for the cakes her mother baked but the honey her father produced and the herbs he grew.

How she'd finished university, spent some months overseas; how a series of catering jobs had finally led her to taking the plunge and starting her own business.

'And that's me up to date,' she said bleakly and added with irony, 'how about you?'

He avoided the question. 'No romantic involvement?'

'Me?' Mia drew her finger around the rim of her glass. 'Not really. Not *seriously*. I haven't had the time. How about you?' she asked again.

'I'm...' He paused and grimaced. 'Actually, I'm currently unattached. Nina—I don't know if you've heard of Nina French?' He raised a dark eyebrow at her.

'Who hasn't?' Mia murmured impatiently. 'Top model, utterly gorgeous, daughter of an ambassador,' she added.

'Yes.' He nodded. 'We had a relationship. It fell through. Today, as a matter of fact.'

Mia choked on a sip of her drink. 'Today?'

He nodded.

'Is that why you were late?' she asked incredulously.

He nodded. 'We had a monumental row just before we were due to set out—to be here on time.' He
shrugged. 'About fifty per cent of our relationship con-
sisted of monumental rows, now I come to think of it.'

'Oh. I'm sorry,' Mia said. 'But that probably means
a…a grand reunion.'

'Not this time,' he replied perfectly coolly, so coolly
it sent a little shiver down Mia's spine.

He was quiet for a time, rolling his glass in his
hands. 'Otherwise,' he continued, 'I've worked like a
Trojan to fill my father's shoes since he had that stroke.
He died a few months ago.'

'I read about that. I'm sorry.'

'Don't be. It was a release—for all of us, I guess.
After the stroke he became embittered and extremely
hard to live with. He was always a hard man. I never
felt I was living up to his expectations before he became ill but even less so afterwards.'

He sat back and tasted his drink. 'I've even branched
out in new directions, successfully, but—' he paused
and shrugged '—I can't help feeling he wouldn't have
approved or that he would have thought of a different
way of doing things.'

'I didn't know him much,' Mia murmured.

'The thing is—' Carlos drained his drink and looked
out into the sunset '—I don't know why I'm telling
you this; maybe weddings generate a desire to understand things—or maybe monumental rows do it—' he
shrugged '—but I don't know if it's thanks to him and
his…lack of enthusiasm for most things, including me,
that's given me a similar outlook on life.'

Mia frowned. 'What do you mean?'

'There's something missing. Hard to put my finger on it, though.'

'Maybe you'd like to take a year off and live amongst some primitive tribe for a change? Is it that kind of an itch?'

He grimaced. 'Not exactly.'

'Then it could be a wife and family you're lacking,' Mia said in a motherly sort of way and was completely unprepared for what came next.

He studied her for a long moment, his eyes narrowed and very intent. Then he said, 'You wouldn't like to take Nina's place?'

Mia's eyes widened and her mouth fell open. 'What do you mean?'

'You wouldn't like to get engaged to me? Not that I was engaged to Nina, but—' He gestured.

She swallowed, choked again on a sip of her drink and came up spluttering.

He eyed her quizzically. 'An unusual reaction,' he murmured.

'No. I mean yes. I mean…how could you?' She reached for a napkin from the trolley and patted her eyes and her mouth. 'I don't think that's funny,' she told him coldly.

He raised a dark eyebrow at her. 'It wasn't meant to be. I'm in rather desperate need of a—what should I call it?—a shield at the moment. From Nina and the whole damn caboodle of them.' He looked irritated to death.

'Them? Who?' Mia queried with a frown.

'The set she moves in, Juanita too, my mother and all

the rest of them.' He gestured. 'You saw them all today.' He paused, then smiled suddenly. 'In comparison, the housekeeper's daughter is like pure sweet spring water.'

Mia moved abruptly and went white to her lips. 'How dare you?' she whispered. 'How dare you patronise me with your ridiculous proposal and think you can make me laugh about being the housekeeper's daughter?'

'Mia—' he sat up '—it may be seven years ago but you and I set each other alight once—remember? Perhaps it didn't mean a great deal to you, but it happened.'

'M-may not have meant m-much to me?' Mia had trouble getting the words out. 'What are you saying?'

'You ran away, remember?'

'I…Carlos, your mother warned me off,' Mia cried, all her unspoken but good intentions not to rake up the past forgotten. 'She told me I could never be the one for you, no "housekeeper's daughter" would be good enough to be your wife. She told me you were only toying with me anyway and she threatened to sack my parents without references if I didn't go away.'

'*What*?' he growled, looking so astounded Mia could only stare at him wide-eyed.

'You didn't know.' It was a statement rather than a question.

'I ended up in hospital that night, remember? When I got home you'd gone. Listen, just tell me how it happened,' he ordered grimly.

Mia stared into the past. 'She came home first, your mother,' she said slowly. 'The storm had passed but I was still—' she hesitated a moment '—I was still lying on the settee. I hadn't heard her. You were asleep. She was…she was livid.' Mia swallowed and shivered. 'She banished me to the service quarters after I'd told her what had happened and she rang for a medevac helicopter. I don't know when you woke up. I don't know if you had concussion but the next day was when she warned me off.'

'What about your parents?'

'I never told them, not what had happened with you. But I had just received an offer of a place at a Queensland university. I hadn't been sure I'd take it—it would mean I'd be a long way from my parents—but that's what I told them—that I'd made up my mind to do it. I left two days later,' she said bleakly. 'You hadn't come back. I didn't even know if you would. But I couldn't risk them losing their jobs.' She looked at him long and steadily. 'Not both of them at the same time. I just couldn't.'

He closed his eyes briefly. 'I'm *sorry*. I had no idea. I must have been quite groggy because I don't remember much about the medevac. But I did go back to West Windward after all sorts of tests and scans and—' he shook his head impatiently '—palaver to determine whether I'd cracked my skull but you'd gone. That was when she told me you'd got a place at a Queensland university, that your parents were so proud of you and what an achievement it was for you. So I congratulated them and *they* told me they were so proud of you and there seemed to be no trauma attached to it.'

Mia patted her eyes again with the napkin. 'They were proud of me.' She shrugged. 'Did you never…' she paused, then looked at him directly '…did you never consider looking for me to check it out?'

He held her gaze for a long moment, then he said, 'No.'

'Why not?' she whispered.

He looked away and rubbed his jaw. Then he looked directly into her eyes. 'Mia, it occurred to me I could only mess up your life. I wasn't ready for a relationship so all I could offer you was an on/off affair, especially if you were up in Queensland. I'd only just taken over from my father so my life was in the process of being completely reorganised.'

He shrugged. 'I could have kicked myself for doing it—' He stopped abruptly as she flinched visibly.

'Hell,' he said. 'I'm *sorry* but—'

But Mia had had enough. She jumped up precipitately. 'So, if your mother hadn't warned me off, *you would have*?'

'No.' He said it decisively and he got to his feet and reached for her. 'No.'

As she jumped away she tripped and would have fallen if he hadn't grabbed her. 'Listen to me,' he ordered as he wound his arms around her. 'Just listen.'

Mia ignored him and struggled to free herself.

'Mia,' he warned, 'since when did you think you could beat me in a damn fight? Be still and listen.'

'There's nothing you can say I want to hear,' she gasped.

He eyed her narrowly, her flushed cheeks and her eyes dark with pain, her hair coming loose. 'OK.' He shrugged. 'Then how about this?'

And before she had a chance to identify what he was leading up to, he bent his head and claimed her mouth with a kiss.

She went limp in his arms, from sheer surprise about the way he did it, the way he moved his hands on her body. The feel of him, steel-hard against her softness, was mesmerising. And her lips parted beneath his because she simply couldn't help herself.

When it was over her head was resting on his arm, her hair flowing over it, her eyes huge, very green and stunned, her lips parted in sheer shock—shock that he had done it, shock that she had responded after his news of what had to amount to a betrayal.

'Don't look like that,' he said.

'Why did you do it?' she whispered.

'It's a traditional way to stop a fight between a man and a woman,' he said dryly. 'Didn't you know?'

Her lashes fell and it occurred to him that he'd hurt her again—like some ham-fisted clod, he thought with distaste. 'Mia, I would never have warned you off because you were the housekeeper's daughter.'

'Oh, Carlos, you may be able to deceive yourself but—'

'Listen,' he broke in savagely, 'yes, I'd have told you there was no future for us *then* but it had nothing to do with who you were. I have never,' he said through his teeth, 'shared my mother's delusions of grandeur.'

It flashed through Mia's mind, an image of herself during the day and how, once again, she'd keenly felt her position on the sidelines, despite her designer clothes and her undoubted skills. How she'd proven to herself today that she still had a long way to go in the self-confidence stakes, how she might always be a fringe-dweller compared to the O'Connors and the ubiquitous Nina French.

But above all how much it *hurt* to know that Carlos would have warned her off himself…

As for his proposal?

'I think you must be mad,' she said with bitter candour, 'if you really believe I'd want to get engaged to you. After all that—have you any idea how cheap your mother made me feel?'

He closed his eyes briefly, then released her and handed her her glass. She blinked and took a sip of brandy.

Carlos stared at her for an eternity, then he said abruptly, 'How old are you now?'

She narrowed her eyes. 'Why?'

'Why not—twenty-five?'

She nodded.

'Has there been *anyone*?'

Two spots of colour entered her cheeks and she put her glass down on the trolley with a snap. 'That's none of your business, Carlos.'

'I think it is. I think it must have been a ghastly experience. My mother—' He gestured and shrugged.

'I'm a little surprised you believe me,' Mia broke in.

'My mother,' he repeated dryly, 'has persistently meddled in all our lives but not in a way that's actually hurt anyone like this before. What happened to my father came as a big shock to her too and may have made her…may have unbalanced her a bit.' He paused and grimaced. 'Whatever, I can't let this go.'

'There's nothing you can do. I…one…gets over these things.'

'That's the problem, I don't think you have. I strongly suspect you're a twenty-five-year-old virgin, Mia.'

Mia gasped and jumped up. 'Will you…will you just go away?' she flung at him. 'To…to think,' she stammered, 'that *I* thought you were the nicest of the O'Connors.'

He lifted a wry eyebrow. 'The best of a bad bunch?'

'Yes! No. Oh!' Mia clenched her fists and ground her teeth and suddenly it was all too much for her again and she kicked her shoes off and ran out onto the veranda, onto the lawn and down towards her cottage.

Of course she came to grief—it was that kind of day.

She didn't see the sliver of glass she stepped onto although she yelped in pain.

Carlos was right behind her, and he said her name on a harsh breath and simply picked her up and turned as if to take her back to the big house.

'No, no,' she said raggedly. 'I don't want to bleed all over the house.'

'Where then?'

'Down there, my cottage. I've got a first aid kit. Oh, I'm bleeding all over *you*.'

'Don't worry about it. Here we are. Stand on one foot while I open the door and get the lights.'

A few minutes later Mia was sitting lengthwise on her settee with a towel under her foot. Carlos had turned all the lights on and, following her instructions, had found the first aid kit in the bathroom.

'I'm a good doctor, by the way,' he said as he laid out tweezers, a bowl of antiseptic, cotton wool and dressings.

'How do you know?' Mia peeled off her stocking.

'I've had no complaints to date.'

'How many people have you actually "doctored"?' she asked. 'Is it deep?'

He studied her heel. 'Deep enough. But I can't see anything in it and we should be able to keep it from bleeding until tomorrow when we can get you to a proper doctor. It might need a couple of stitches. You'll have to keep off it for a while.'

He dabbed it liberally with cotton wool dipped in antiseptic, then he dried it and applied a dressing.

'There.' He sat back. Then he reached for her and took her in his arms. 'And you're a good patient,' he said into her hair. 'Feeling OK?' He held her away and studied her face. 'You look a bit pale.'

Mia grimaced and, without giving it a second thought, laid her head against his shoulder. 'I'll be OK. I feel a bit stupid. I always check the lawn for broken glass; when people drink you never know what they can end up doing with their glasses. I *never* sprint across it barefoot.'

'Why did you?' He kissed the top of her head and it felt like the most natural thing in the world to Mia.

But she sighed. 'I was running away from you, Carlos.' She lifted her head and looked him in the eye. 'For a few minutes I really hated you. And thinking back makes me feel that way again.'

'Then don't think back,' he advised and traced the outline of her mouth. 'It always was one of the most delicious mouths I've ever seen.'

Mia was conscious of a growing clamour in her nerve-endings, delicious but at the same time disturbing, as her awareness of him grew. Awareness of how surprisingly strong he was; he'd carried her with ease. Awareness of all the old sensations being in his arms could arouse, the feel of his body against hers, the pure male scent she used to love so much when they rode together, of the cotton of his shirt mingled with a hint of musk.

Awareness and memories of his hands, so sure when he'd kissed and touched her tonight and once before, even if he was suffering from a concussion on that occasion.

It was that last thought that brought her up with a start. She had to remember that Carlos was dangerous to her mental health!

Correspondingly, she pushed herself away from him and changed tack deliberately and completely. 'This accident couldn't have happened at a worse time. I've got wall-to-wall functions over the next week. I really need to be on my feet!'

'Tomorrow?' he queried.

'No, not tomorrow but from the day after.'

He looked at her with some irony. 'Don't you have any contingency plans? Are yours the only pair of feet available?'

Mia sank back. 'Well, no. There's Gail.'

'Ah, Gail,' Carlos murmured with a sudden glint of amusement in his grey eyes. 'Now, I met Gail. She very kindly introduced herself to me and offered me any assistance I might need.'

Mia looked briefly heavenward.

Carlos noted this with a twist to his lips. 'I did form the impression, however, that, despite being young and impressionable, Gail is a fairly practical person. Possibly a hard worker as well.'

Mia closed her eyes on her inward irritation, then opened them to say honestly, 'You're right. Forgive me, Gail,' she added in an aside.

'So you can give the orders and Gail can carry them out. Problem solved.'

Mia cast him a glance liberally laced with a mixture of frustration and exasperation and, in lieu of being able to trust her voice, merely nodded.

Carlos contemplated her for a long moment, then he said, 'I see.'

Mia blinked. 'What? What do you see?'

'It's not visible to the naked eye.'

She blinked again. 'How do you see it then?'

'It wasn't that kind of an "I see".' He stood up and gathered the first aid accoutrements together and took them to the bathroom. 'It denoted understanding,' he said, coming back.

Mia made a kittenish sound of frustration. '*Understanding of what*?'

'Your state of mind. I get the impression mine is the last advice you'd want to take,' he said with a flourish. 'That kind of understanding.' He moved into the kitchen area. 'Would there be anything to eat in your establishment, Miss Gardiner?'

Mia, who didn't at that moment know whether to laugh or cry—laugh because he could be so crazy at times, cry because he read her so well—said faintly, 'Look in the fridge,' and swallowed a lump in her throat. 'Uh...I'm sorry, I did bleed all over you but cold water is good for getting blood out.'

'You don't say?' He looked down at himself and swore softly. 'I see what you mean. OK, I'll scrub what I can.'

She had to laugh when, after he'd washed the blood-stains away, he found her apron hanging on a hook on the wall and donned it.

'There.' He smoothed it down. 'Presentable.' He opened the fridge door and apparently approved of what he saw. He withdrew a bowl of pasta marinara already prepared and just requiring heating up. There was a small salad also made and under cling wrap.

Lastly he took out a bottle of white wine with a shrug. 'Is there any point in being virtuous *and* sober at this end of the day?'

'Virtuous?' she queried.

'You could hardly call us decadent.'

'Well, no.' Mia paused as Carlos put the pasta in the microwave and set out some cutlery on her little round kitchen table.

Within minutes they were eating and sharing some of the wine.

Mia ate from a tray on her knees; she was still ensconced on the settee with her feet up. They talked desultorily—he was the one who'd promoted the conversation by asking her some questions about the reception business.

'So,' he said at one point, helping himself to more pasta, 'in the case of a bridal party like today, you actually provide a hairdresser and a make-up person so all the dressing et cetera takes place up here—very sensible. It'd be a long drive all kitted out in a wedding dress. But how do the brides cope with a strange hairdresser? I had a girlfriend once who left me to follow her hairdresser to Townsville.'

Mia wound her last mouthful of pasta around her fork and couldn't help grinning. 'The hairdressers and make-up girls work in salons in Sydney, so the bridal party have a couple of appointments with them *before* the big day to work out hairstyles and so on.'

He looked at her with admiration. 'That's pretty inspired, Miss Gardiner.'

She shrugged. 'It's just a question of—' she paused and looked thoughtful '—of helping Mount Wilson to work its magic, I guess.'

'Mmm…' He pushed his bowl away and got up to take the tray from her. 'Who owns the place?'

She told him and then, unwittingly, voiced her concern. 'They're in their eighties now,' she said slowly, 'and they seem to be going downhill a bit. They're getting forgetful and—I guess it's only natural but I think they're worried about Bellbird. They have a nephew who's their heir. He wants them to sell it and invest the money where they'd get a higher return. Of course—'

she gestured '—it's entirely up to them but I might be looking for somewhere else one day. Which would be a pity but—we'll see.'

'Are you attached to the property?' he asked after a moment. 'It's not only a business proposition for you?'

Mia sighed and reached for her wine glass. 'I love it,' she said dreamily and with a faraway look in her eyes. 'I'd love to own it. I'd love to pretend I was a lady from another era who had this summer residence in the hills and a garden I could open to the public if the whim took me. I'd love to call this place home.' She looked at Carlos, smiling. 'Mount Wilson residents can because they have roots here; they have a bit of history behind them.' She smiled at her glass and drained her wine. 'Yes, I think I'd love to play ladies up here at Bellbird. I'd also love to have ten kids.'

He blinked at her. 'Ten?'

She waved a hand. 'No, not really, but some. I love kids.'

She paused and recalled one of her early fantasies— having Carlos's children. She grimaced inwardly but, as had happened to her before, she couldn't help wondering if she ever would have kids now, if she couldn't fall in love again.

'I think maybe it was because I was an only child— that's why a large family appeals. It shouldn't,' she said humorously. 'The last picnic day I had nearly ruined me.'

'Picnic day?' he queried.

'Twice a year I invite some kids from a youth club in an inner city area up for a picnic—well, a sausage sizzle really. Eight- to ten-year-olds. The last lot were especially spirited. They…um…ran riot, you could say. That's what Bill said, anyway.' Her eyes glinted with laughter. 'He also said if he'd ever seen a bunch of hoodlums in the making they were it.'

'Bill?'

'Oh, didn't I mention him? He's the gardener. He and I have a…difficult relationship, although he's a wonderful gardener. It's just that I rather fancy myself as a gardener too.' She shrugged. 'At least my father thought I had green fingers and if anyone should have known, he would have.'

Carlos was sitting in one of her ladder-back kitchen chairs. He had his hands behind his head and was tilting the chair. 'That's…quite a daydream,' he said after a long moment.

Mia dimpled. 'Daydream being the operative word. But I guess we all have daydreams.'

'Yes.' He sounded distracted and almost as if he was examining his daydreams and not finding them satisfactory or perhaps not finding any at all.

'Do you have any…well, ambitions or future plans, if not daydreams?' Mia heard herself asking curiously.

He thought for a long moment with a frown in his eyes. 'I have one,' he said at last. 'Not so much an ambition but one thing I keep a long-term eye on, you could say. Someone I would hate to see steal a march on me.'

'That sounds more like a vendetta than an ambition,' Mia commented. 'Who?'

'Talbot Spencer.'

She blinked. '*The* Talbot Spencer?'

He looked at her dryly. 'Is there another? Yes, him.'

'But he's a builder, like you. I mean…I don't mean you actually build things with your hands these days but his is also a multi-million dollar construction company, isn't it?'

'It is and we've been competing against each other for contracts for years. He's also tried to buy me out a couple of times. That's one reason why I have a thing about him.'

'He's a playboy, isn't he?' Mia frowned as she ran through her mental resources on the subject of Talbot Spencer. Then her eyes widened. 'I suppose you could be called one too, though.'

'Thank you, Mia,' he said sardonically.

'Well—' she gestured '—cars, boats, planes, horses and women. You both seem to qualify.' She paused and pictured Talbot Spencer in her mind's eye, not that she'd ever met him but she'd seen him pictured. Not quite as tall as Carlos and fair-haired, he was still interesting-looking.

'So what was the real needle between the two of you? The cut-throat world of business?'

Carlos leant his chin on his hand and he took so long about it she thought he wasn't going to answer, then he said, 'A woman.'

Mia's lips parted. 'He stole a…a girlfriend from you?'

Carlos shook his head. 'Not from me; it was my best friend's girl. Talbot's a few years older. My friend and I were still at university, whereas he was a seasoned bachelor. She was at uni too. She fell for him and gave my friend his marching orders.' He fiddled with the tablecloth. 'She was a country, convent-schooled girl. Anyway, to cut a long story short, Talbot got her pregnant, paid for her abortion and turned his back on her.'

'Oh, no,' Mia murmured.

'Oh, yes. She was devastated and guilt-ridden over the abortion and she tried to end it all. It took years for her mental scars to heal and my friend went through the mill with her. For which I will never forgive Talbot and he knows it and he knows why. That's why he'd like to grind O'Connor Construction into the ground… Why the hell am I telling you this, Mia?'

She had to smile. 'I don't know. It's been quite a day, one way and another. Maybe that's why.'

'You're not wrong. Uh…where's the bedroom?'

Mia waved a hand in the direction of the loft. 'Up there.'

He stood up. 'That's the only one?'

She nodded.

'Mind if I take a look?'

Mia tried to remember how tidy she'd left her loft, then shrugged. 'Go ahead.'

Five minutes later he looked down at her. 'It's going to be me up here, you down there, Miss Gardiner. Tell me what you need and I'll bring it down.'

Mia sat bolt upright. 'What do you mean? You can't be serious!'

'But I am.'

'Carlos—'

'Mia—' he interrupted firmly '—you cannot honestly expect me to abandon you up here on the top of a mountain with not a soul within reach. How come you live so alone like this in the first place?' he asked irritably.

'I don't. There's another cottage where Bill and his wife live, but she's away at the mo...' She broke off and bit her lip.

'Away at the moment?' he supplied.

Mia nodded.

'Then you're going to have to put up with me because probably the furthest you'll be able to go is hop to the bathroom. There's no way you're going to be able to get up this ladder, for starters.'

And, so saying, he tossed down a pair of pyjamas for her plus a pillow and a duvet.

Mia drew a deep breath as she gathered what he'd thrown down. 'All right, maybe I couldn't do that but otherwise I can manage. Thank you very much for the offer, though; it's really kind of you but I don't need it.'

'Mia...' He came down the ladder and sat on the end of the settee. 'Mia,' he repeated, 'I'm not going to ravish you or even seduce you. Believe me.'

They stared at each other until she said tonelessly, 'I didn't think you were. I just don't like feeling beholden—to anyone.'

'Or are you afraid that even if we're not into ravishment and seduction,' he said dryly, 'you might get to liking me again?'

Mia opened her mouth but Long John Silver chose that moment to make his presence felt. He neighed shrilly several times.

Mia's hand flew to her mouth.

'Your horse?' Carlos queried.

'Yes. I forgot all about him! He hasn't been fed or rugged or put in his stall for the night. Oh!' She made to swing her legs down but sanity prevailed. 'I'm not going to be able to do it, am I?' she said hollowly.

'No.' Carlos got up. 'But I can. I can also get some more wood for the fire.'

'What about…aren't you staying with friends, though? Won't they be wondering where you are?'

He pulled a mobile from his pocket. 'I'll ring them. Any more objections?' he asked with sudden impatience.

She lay back with a sigh. 'No.' She sat up immediately, though, with anxiety etched into her expression. 'Be careful with Long John. He can bite.'

'Surely you don't put up with that?' Carlos raised an incredulous eyebrow at her.

'Oh, not me,' Mia assured him. 'Usually only strangers. Well, Bill, but I wouldn't be surprised if Bill provokes him.'

'Thanks for the warning,' he said dryly. 'Anything else I need to be warned about? Like killer cats or pet snakes in the loft?'

She had to laugh. 'No. Oh…' She grimaced and hesitated.

'Spill it,' he ordered briefly.

'Well, I didn't lock up. The main house, I mean. Not that we usually have any crime up here, but I don't like to leave it all open.'

'Just tell me what to do. Come to think of it, I left my car unlocked.'

Mia explained how to lock up the house.

'Wish me luck,' he said wryly and stepped out into the night.

Mia stared at the closed door and was conscious of never feeling more confused.

Bewitched, bothered and bewildered, she thought, and closed her eyes. How could she possibly kiss Carlos O'Connor when he had admitted there had never been a future for them?

A few minutes later she decided to take advantage of his absence and she got up painfully and hopped to the bathroom.

When she got back to the settee she was colourfully arrayed in her tartan pyjamas and she snuggled under the duvet.

Perhaps the wine on top of a couple of brandies was helping to dull the pain in her heel, she reflected, but it wasn't too bad.

Her last thought was that it certainly wasn't going to keep her awake and she fell asleep without intending to, without even realising it, on a day of mixed emotions like no other in her life.

Carlos came back eventually, all chores done, but Mia didn't even stir when he added some wood to the stove.

He stood looking down at her for a long time. At the almost ridiculously long lashes against her cheeks. At her thick dark hair that she'd braided, making her look younger, as did—he smiled—the tartan pyjamas. At her mouth—it *was* one of the most luscious mouths he'd seen and if he looked at it long enough it was hard not to want to kiss it.

What would happen if he did kiss that delicious mouth again right now? Lightly at first at the same time as he stroked her cheek.

Would she sigh a warm little puff of air, then reach out to wind her arms around his neck? Would she invite him to lie beside her and accept his hands on her body in all those softly rounded or slender places?

He moved restlessly and shoved his hands in his pockets as he was struck by the irony of it, this compulsion that came over him from time to time to have and to hold Mia.

He gritted his teeth but pulled up a kitchen chair and continued to watch her as she slept.

Truth be told, he was having trouble linking the two Mias—the one from his past and this one. Although he remembered clearly being aware of the shy schoolgirl crush she'd had on him he'd ignored it, quite sure it would go away but, before it had happened, a freak storm had intervened, he'd got clobbered on the head by a falling branch and when he wasn't sure what was what, he'd been beset by the certainty that all he wanted was to have and to hold Mia Gardiner.

Then sanity and reality had returned and he'd come back to West Windward kicking himself, although still not a hundred per cent sure what had actually happened between them.

Only to find the problem was solved. Mia apparently had accepted that he'd been concussed and gone on her way to a Queensland university, making her parents very proud.

But it hadn't happened like that, he reminded himself grimly.

How had she managed to throw off as much of the shadow of it all as she had?

He thought of his mother with grim forbearance. Arancha was—Arancha, fiercely loyal to her family, no matter the cost and no matter—he grimaced—how misplaced her sentiments might be.

It was a problem that had escalated with his father's death, one he'd inherited. It had struck him once or twice that maybe grandchildren would be the balm Arancha needed, only to wonder with a touch of black humour what kind of chaos his mother could create as an interfering grandmother.

Fortunately Juanita stood little nonsense from her mother but could Damien stand up to her? Come to that, Juanita stood little nonsense from Damien, he reflected wryly, and wondered if his new brother-in-law had understood what he was getting himself into.

None of which, it occurred to him, was of any help to him in this contretemps. How could he make it up to Mia for his mother's cruelty? Not only that, but *his* thoughtless declaration today that he could have kicked himself for what he'd done. And the admission that he would have deemed it right to warn her off too? Not only all that, but not checking out with her that she was all right seven years ago.

Yes, she might have made a success of her life but, beneath that, there obviously lurked the stigma of being branded 'the housekeeper's daughter'. And it was obvious that it still hurt.

What about the attraction there had been between them? Maybe only a teenage crush on her part and a concussion-fuelled moment of madness on his but there all the same. Yet, once again he'd held her and kissed her and she'd responded.

He studied her with a frown, sleeping so peacefully and looking quite unlike the high-powered executive she was in reality.

It must take considerable organisational skills and flair to hold receptions on Mount Wilson. The logistics alone—just about everything had to come from Sydney—were mind-boggling.

Not only that, the foresight to appreciate that the special magic of the mountain would make it irresistible to people for their special days. So, yes, it wasn't inappropriate to call her a high-powered executive.

Even though she slept in tartan pyjamas and looked about sixteen when she did.

He stretched and at the same time felt his mobile phone vibrate in his pocket. He took it out and studied it.

Nina…

He switched it off and put it back in his pocket.

Gorgeous, exotic Nina who ticked all the right boxes for his mother. Model looks, father an ex-politician rewarded for his services with an ambassadorship, uncle married to an Englishwoman who was a Lady in her own right.

Nina, who could be the essence of warmth and charm or cool and regal depending on how the mood took her. Nina, who aroused in most men the desire to bed her, yet who could be incredibly, screamingly insecure.

He stared at the flickering shadows on the wall behind the settee and listened to the crackle of the fire.

What was he going to do about Nina?

She was the one who'd called off their relationship in the middle of the row—he couldn't even remember how it had started now—they'd had before Juanita's wedding.

Well, yes, he could remember, he realised, not exactly how it had started but what it had been about. It was something that had been brewing through all of Juanita's wedding preparations. It all had to do with Nina's desire that *they* get married, something he'd not, for reasons all too clear, although belatedly to him, been willing to do.

And yet he'd allowed things between them to carry on when he'd known he shouldn't but his pride had got in the way.

He'd allowed the good times to define their relationship and he'd cut himself off from her when she was being impossible—she always came back to him as if he was the only spar she had to cling to in the storm-tossed sea of life. He had no doubt that was what she was ringing him for.

But could they go on like this?

He lowered his gaze to the girl sleeping so peacefully on her settee. And he was reminded suddenly of the ridiculous proposal he'd made to her—that she take Nina's place. What had prompted that? he wondered.

Could he blame her for being angry and insulted by it? No...

But what germ of an idea or perception had prompted him even to think it?

The feeling that Mia wouldn't cling, she wouldn't employ emotional blackmail to hold him? That she wouldn't be impossibly nice in between being a bundle of bizarre hang-ups?

If anyone should have some bizarre hang-ups, Mia Gardiner should, he reflected, directly due to the behaviour of himself and his mother.

CHAPTER THREE

MIA WOKE THE next morning to the sound of running water.

She moved under her duvet but she was so snug and comfortable, apart from a slight throbbing in her foot, she was reluctant to get up, reluctant even to open her eyes.

As for the water she was hearing, could it be rain? They had been forecasting rain for a few days…

But no, it didn't sound like rain on the roof, it sounded just like her shower.

Her lashes flew open and she sat up with a gasp as it all came tumbling back into her mind. It had to be Carlos in her shower.

Right on cue, she heard the bathroom door open and he padded through the kitchen wearing only his khaki trousers and drying his hair with a towel.

'Morning,' he said. 'Do you happen to have a razor I could borrow?'

She blinked. 'Only a tiny one. I get my legs waxed.'

He rubbed the dark shadows on his jaw. 'Then you'll

have to put up with me like this. What's your favourite tipple first thing in the morning?'

Her eyes widened. 'Tipple?'

'Champagne? Vodka and fresh orange juice? I personally subscribe to a Bloody Mary.'

He dropped the towel and reached for his shirt lying over a chair. 'You believed me, didn't you?' He shook his head. 'No wonder you're so suspicious if you harbour these dissipated views of me.'

Mia closed her mouth and tried to dampen her look of no doubt naive surprise. Then she confessed with a grimace that she had believed him for a moment. 'But I gather you meant tea or coffee? If so, tea, please, black, no sugar and one slice of raisin toast with butter.'

'Done,' he replied, pulling his shirt off after realising it was inside out. 'Mind you, there are times when champagne is a great way to toast in the morning.'

Foolishly, she realised too late, Mia raised an eyebrow at him. 'When?'

He studied her, his lips twisting. 'When a man and a woman have a night to remember, to celebrate.' His grey eyes flicked over her in a way that left her in no doubt he was visualising a night to remember with her.

Mia blushed—it felt as if from her toes to the top of her head. And hard as she tried to tear her gaze away from his, she couldn't do it as wave after wave of colour ran through her and her senses were alive and leaping. 'Oh.'

'That hadn't occurred to you, obviously,' he said with a glint of wicked amusement in his eyes now.

'No,' she said slowly, but her thoughts were running

riot. She had to get a grip on her responses to him! 'It may not be standard behaviour for housekeepers or their daughters,' she told him tartly.

He frowned. 'You really do have a chip on your shoulder, don't you, Mia?'

She bit her lip but decided she might as well soldier on. 'Yes,' she said starkly and pushed aside the duvet. 'But I don't want to discuss it, thank you, Carlos. I would *really* like to go to the bathroom.'

He put down his shirt again. 'Sure.' And, before she had time to resist, not that she would have been able to anyway, he came across, picked her up and deposited her outside the bathroom door.

Mia ground her teeth but was at a loss to be able to do anything about it.

He still didn't have his shirt on when she made her way out of the bathroom, but there was a steaming cup of black tea and a slice of raisin toast waiting for her on a tray. There was also a neat pile of clothes on the settee. A pair of jeans and a T-shirt as well as a selection of underwear.

'Don't,' he warned as he saw her eyeing the undies with a pink tinge of embarrassment creeping into her cheeks.

'Don't what?' she managed.

'Don't be embarrassed or go all prim and proper on me,' he elucidated. 'I've seen a few bras and panties in my time so I'm not going to become all excited and leap on you.'

'Ah.'

He eyed her. 'And there's still no way you could have gone up the ladder.'

Mia changed tack mentally and said sweetly, 'Thank you, Mr O'Connor.'

He looked surprised for a moment, then picked up his shirt but clicked his tongue as he stared at it.

'What?' Mia asked through a mouthful of toast.

'More blood on it!' He took it over to the sink and rinsed one of the sleeves.

'I'm doubly sorry,' Mia said, actually managing to sound quite contrite as she sipped her tea.

He looked across the kitchen at her with a spark of curiosity in his eyes. 'If that's what a sip of tea and a slice of toast can do for you I'm tempted to think a full breakfast could work miracles.'

Mia had to laugh. 'I don't know about that but I do love my first cuppa.'

He rinsed his shirt sleeve, squeezed it out and turned it right side out again.

That was when Mia frowned as she stared at his back. Her gaze had been drawn to it anyway because she'd suddenly been possessed of an irrational desire to be in a position to run her hands up and down the powerful lines and sleek muscles of it.

'Hang on,' she said slowly. 'What have *you* done to yourself? Your back—there's a black and blue patch on your back.'

'Ah.' He squinted over his shoulder. 'Can't see it but that wasn't me, that was your blasted horse.'

Mia's hand flew to her mouth. 'But I warned you.'

'And I told him I'd been forewarned and he'd be stupid to try anything.' He raked his hair with his fingers. 'We obviously don't speak the same language.'

Mia started to laugh helplessly. 'I'm sorry. I'm sorry,' she repeated. 'I know it's not funny—'

'You expect me to believe that?' he broke in politely.

'You know what I mean! But anyway, you'd better let me put something on it.'

He brought his own tea over and sat down on the coffee table. 'Don't worry about me. Let's see your foot.'

Mia was still shaken by giggles but she stuck her foot out obediently. He unwound the bandage and lifted the dressing off carefully.

'Hmm...still bleeding a bit. Look, I'm going to my friends' to get a change of clothes, then I'll be back and I'll take you to the nearest clinic.'

'You don't have to.'

He got up to fetch the first aid kit. 'Don't start, Mia,' he warned over his shoulder. 'By the way, it's raining.'

Mia glanced out of the window and rubbed her face as she noted the grey, gloomy view. 'I thought it was earlier. At least we don't have a function on today.'

'At least,' he agreed.

They were both silent while he redressed her foot until she said out of the blue, 'We always seem to be bandaging each other.'

He looked up. 'I was just thinking the same thing. History repeats itself.'

'What...what would your father have thought if you'd married someone like me?'

He frowned. 'What makes you ask that?'

'You said his influence was a sort of negative one. Do you know why he was like that?'

Carlos smiled, a tigerish little smile. 'I think it had something to do with the fact that he'd done all the hard work, he'd built the company up from the dirt, whereas I'd, to his mind, had it easy. The right schools, university, the means to—' he gestured '—do whatever I wanted.'

Mia thought for a moment. 'That doesn't mean to say you couldn't be an achiever. It looks as if you've nurtured his dreams and his company and taken them on to even greater heights.'

He shrugged. 'Yes, I have. I doubt if even that would have given him much pleasure.' He looked into space for a moment. 'I don't see why you're wondering about this in connection with us.' He searched her expression narrowly.

'I wondered if he'd disinherit you if he didn't approve of whoever you married.'

'I've no doubt he'd have found something to disapprove of, whoever it was.' He paused and looked into the distance with his eyes narrowed as if some chord had been struck with him but he didn't elaborate.

'Why do people get like that?' Mia asked.

He linked his fingers. 'I think it's the struggle. The almighty battle to pull yourself up by your bootstraps. Coupled probably with a sense of ambition that's like a living force.' He looked down at his hands. 'I could be wrong. But no, he wouldn't have disinherited me. That's the other thing that…weighed, you could say, with my father—my mother.'

Mia blinked. 'How do you mean?'

'She would never have stood by and let him disinherit me.' He grimaced. 'I'm not sure he entirely appreciated the fact that, while she would defend him with her dying breath, she would do the same for me. She's very strong on family loyalty.'

Mia stared into space and listened to the rain on the roof. Then she shivered.

'Mia, what exactly happened that night?'

Her startled gaze jerked back to his. 'You don't remember?' she breathed incredulously.

'I remember…feeling like hell and suddenly being possessed of the strongest urge to hold you in my arms. As if it would make me feel a whole lot better. It did.' His lips twisted. 'Then I remember laughing about something but not exactly what it was and—'

'You called me a pilchard,' she broke in.

He blinked. 'Why the hell would I do that?'

'You actually told me to stop wriggling around like a trapped pilchard.'

Mia said it seriously and her expression was grave but she couldn't maintain it as the expression in his grey eyes went from puzzled to incredulous then gleamed with laughter.

'I'm surprised you didn't find a pilchard to clobber me with! Hopefully I retrieved things?'

'You called me a siren next. Then you kissed me.'

'I remember that.' His gaze fell to her mouth and Mia trembled inwardly. 'But that's all,' he said after a long moment.

A moment when her fingertips tingled as if she was

actually touching them to his skin, as if she was running her fingers through the night-darkness of his hair and trailing them along the blue shadows of his jaw.

If she did that, would he grasp her wrist and kiss her knuckles, would he flick open the buttons of her tartan pyjama top and touch her breasts?

The mere thought of it made her nipples harden and a rush of heat run through her body. She moved restlessly and said hurriedly, 'That is all.'

'Nothing else?' he asked, scanning her pink cheeks with a frown.

'No. You fell asleep and I just stayed there. I didn't want to wake you.' She gestured. 'To be honest, I didn't want to move. I think I must have dozed too because I didn't hear your mother drive in.' She hesitated. 'Why do you ask?'

'So it was only a kiss and an embrace?'

She stared at him. 'Did you think there was...' her voice shook '...more?'

'Not as I remembered it, but...' He frowned. 'For you to be so upset and still so affected by it, I'm now wondering.'

Mia drew a vast agitated breath. 'You think I've made a mountain out of a molehill?'

'No.' He closed his eyes briefly and took her hands.

She wrested them free. 'You do. Oh, will you just go away and leave me in peace, Carlos O'Connor? To think that I once thought I had a crush on you—'

She broke off and her hand flew to her mouth.

'It's all right. I knew.' He stood up—and someone knocked on the door.

'You decent, Mia?' Bill James called out. 'I'm home, just thought to let you know—oh!' He stopped abruptly as Carlos swept open the door.

Bill was in his sixties, white-haired, stocky, tanned and with a distinctly roman nose. His bushy white eyebrows all but disappeared beneath his cap as he took in every detail of the scene before him.

Mia in her pyjamas, Carlos just starting to pull his sweatshirt on.

'Blimey,' he said. 'I'm sorry. I had no idea. I'll go.'

'I'll come with you,' Carlos said. 'I've just been given my marching orders. See you later, Mia. Think you can manage in the meantime?'

'Yes,' Mia said through her teeth, then was forced to back down somewhat. 'Uh...my horse. He needs a feed. Bill, would you mind? Just be careful—'

'Tell you what, Mia,' Bill broke in, 'it's time you got rid of that horse—he's a menace.'

'I couldn't agree with you more.' Carlos put out his hand and introduced himself to Bill, and they left together as if they were lifelong friends, closing the door behind them.

Mia stared after them, then picked up her pillow and hurled it at the door.

'I can't believe you've done all this,' Mia said later as the sports car nosed its way into Bellbird's driveway and pulled up at the main house. It was pouring.

'Taken you to the doctor?' Carlos raised a quizzical eyebrow. 'Would you rather I'd left you to bleed to death?'

Mia clicked her tongue. 'I wasn't going to!'

'The slightest pressure and it was still bleeding,' he commented.

Mia looked down at her bandaged foot. She now had three stitches in her heel and she had a crutch.

'No, not that. Thank you very much for that,' she said stiffly. 'I obviously couldn't have driven myself. No, I mean ringing Gail last night so—'

'Look, Mia,' he said evenly, 'when I came to lock up last night I noticed Gail's number in a prominent position on the wall in your study and I decided the sooner she knew you were incapacitated the better. I was going to tell you when I got back to the cottage but you were fast asleep. What's wrong with that?'

'Gail,' Mia said precisely, 'will be absolutely agog to think that you spent the night with me and will be imagining all sorts of wild and improbable things. You don't know her. She is also incapable of keeping things to herself so it will be all over the mountain. And Bill is just as bad,' she added forcefully.

'Who cares?' Carlos replied this time. 'You and I know the truth, that's all that matters, and anyway, in this day and age, nobody thinks twice about that kind of stuff. OK. I presume you will want to see Gail?'

Mia nodded.

'Then we'll do this the easy way.'

She looked questioningly at him but he simply got out of the car and came to open her door. He then scooped her out of the seat and carried her into the house. 'You know, if I owned this place,' he remarked at the same time, 'I'd add some undercover parking. Your office?' he asked.

'Yes. Oh, hi, Gail,' she added. 'And you remember Mr O'Connor?'

'Mia!' Gail said dramatically as she fluttered around them. 'Are you all right? Mr O'Connor, good to see you again. Bring her this way, Mr O'Connor—I've put a cushion under her desk for her to put her foot on and I've made some coffee. I'm sure we could all do with some!'

It was over lunch that Mia asked, 'Gail, are you sure you can handle all this? You'll have to do everything I normally do for the next few days as well as the stuff you usually do.'

Gail hesitated. 'There is my sister, Kylie. She's only fourteen but she's pretty good around the house. I'm sure she could help and she's on school holidays at the moment.'

'Kylie!' Mia sat up. 'That's brilliant. Will your mum mind?'

'No way. Anything to take Kylie's mind off boys at the moment will be very welcome.' Gail cast her gaze skywards as if she was at least forty with a boy-mad daughter of her own.

'All right.' Mia selected a smoked salmon sandwich. 'Thanks for making lunch, Gail.'

'No problemo.' Gail poured their tea. 'Uh—is Mr O'Connor coming back?'

'He didn't say—rather, all he said was, "I'll be back". By the way, Gail—' Mia took a sip of tea '—I misled you a bit yesterday. My parents used to work for the O'Connors, that's how I knew about Juanita and her family.'

Gail put the teapot down slowly. 'So you used to know him?' she said.

'Yes.' Mia flinched inwardly to see Gail staring at her with patent, revamped curiosity and regretted embarking on these tangled explanations. She'd only done so because she'd felt guilty about not precisely lying to Gail the day before but not being exactly honest and open either. Had she also thought it mightn't look so bad, the fact that Carlos had spent the night in the cottage with her, if they knew each other?

She bit her lip and could have kicked herself but decided she had to soldier on. 'I was only the housekeeper's daughter and I didn't think they'd recognise me. That's why—' She broke off and shrugged.

'So that's why he came back after the wedding was over,' Gail said slowly. 'How lucky was that? I mean your foot.'

I only cut my foot because he antagonised me enough to make me run away from him, Mia thought but did not say. 'Yes. Yes, it was lucky,' she murmured.

'You know what?' Gail rearranged her teacup and saucer, 'I think he'll keep coming back,' she confided.

Mia looked at her uneasily. 'Oh, I don't know about that.'

'I do.' Gail smiled mysteriously. 'But I won't say another word.'

'Gail!' Mia stared at her assistant with deep frustration written large into her expression. 'You can't just say things like that and leave them up in the air.'

'OK, if you want it spelt out.' Gail got up as if she thought she might have to take evasive action. 'There's chemistry,' she announced.

'What?' Mia frowned.

'There's a little crackle of tension in you when he's around and he enjoys picking you up and carrying you around. Not only that, he enjoys the fact that it annoys you. I can see a wicked little glint in his eye when he does it.'

Mia stared at her assistant open-mouthed.

'You did want to know, didn't you?' Gail enquired, looking the picture of injured innocence.

'Yes. No. You're quite wrong, Gail. I—'

But with a perky, 'We'll see!' over her shoulder, Gail left the office.

Mia glared after her. Next she glared at the last salmon sandwich on the plate but decided to eat it anyway. Then she sat back with a deep sigh, feeling moody and without grace.

Of course being confined to hopping around on one foot, even with a crutch—which was not that easy to manage—was enough to make her feel helpless but it was also an emotional helplessness. It was like a roller coaster ride.

What had she believed would happen between her and Carlos all those years ago?

At the time she'd had no expectations, it had all happened out of the blue and—yes, she had to concede, she'd wondered if it was all due to his concussion. But she'd also thought it wasn't impossible for him to be attracted to her.

Then had come the horrible confrontation with Arancha, and the weeks after she'd left West Windward when she'd cherished the little seed of hope in her heart that Carlos would find her and tell her his mother was wrong, he needed her, he wanted her, he loved her.

But as the weeks had grown into a month, then two, and she'd felt that fragile little seed die and she'd... hated him?

No, she thought, that was the funny part about it. If anything, she'd hated herself because she couldn't hate him, although she'd certainly hated his mother.

But the other funny thing was when she'd refused to allow herself to wallow in self-pity and started living again, socialising and dating and so on, it didn't happen for her. There had been no real attractions and the half-baked ones she'd thought might turn into the real thing never had. And that was down to Carlos.

'OK.' Gail came into the office, delving into her purse for her car keys.

Carlos had not returned after dropping Mia off from the doctor, although he'd said he'd be back and he'd stay the night. Consequently, Mia had asked Gail to make up two of the never used bedrooms in the main house.

Gail had cast her a narrowed look and said, 'Much snugger in the cottage, but it's up to you.'

'Yes,' Mia had replied with something of a snap.

'Look, I'm sorry I've got to go before he gets back,' Gail said now as she jangled her keys, 'but everything is under control and Bill is here. It's not such a big event tomorrow, only thirty for lunch, a garden club on their annual day out so they'll be raving about this garden—and I'll bring Kylie with me to lend a hand. Sure you'll be OK? I would stay until he comes but it's my Girl Guides night tonight so I can't be late.'

'I'm fine, promise, don't worry. And I've plenty of bookwork to occupy me.' Mia leant over her desk and touched Gail's hand. 'Thanks, pal. I don't know what I'd do without you!'

Gail beamed with pleasure.

Mia sat back and listened to her drive off, then smote her forehead with the heel of her hand because she'd been going to ask Gail to feed Long John Silver and put him away for the night but she'd forgotten. Gail was good with Long John.

Only a moment or so later, however, she heard a car drive up and assumed it would be Carlos, but frowned suddenly because his car had a distinctive engine note. She discovered she was right; it wasn't Carlos, it was her neighbour, Ginny Castle, and her twelve-year-old son Harry.

'Come in, Ginny,' Mia called in response to Ginny's knock. 'In the study.'

Ginny, a bustling redhead, came through, talking nineteen-to-the-dozen, as was her habit.

'Just heard you've got stitches in your foot, Mia, love—you really should be more careful!—but anyway, with Bill and Lucy away, how about if we took Long John home until you're up to scratch again? Harry can ride him over and I can bring all his clobber in the ute.'

'Ginny, you're a darling!' Mia said with very real gratitude. 'I was going to ask Gail to feed and rug him before she left but she was obviously in a hurry and anyway, I forgot. And actually Bill is home, but he and Long John don't get along.'

'Not a problem. Got anyone to feed and water *you*?' Ginny asked and laughed richly.

'Someone is coming, thanks all the same.'

'Then we'll get going before it gets dark.' And she shepherded Harry out in front of her.

'Just be careful, Harry,' Mia called. 'He can bite.'

Harry evaded his mama and stuck his head back round the office door. 'Not me, he doesn't!'

'How come?' Mia enquired.

'Because the last time he tried it I bit him back. See you, Mia.'

Mia was still laughing and experiencing a warm glow a few minutes later when the phone rang.

She answered it but when she put it down many minutes later she was pale and shaken-looking and she dropped her head into her hands.

'What's wrong?'

She jumped and realised Carlos must have driven in without her hearing him. It was raining again. He stood in the doorway in jeans and a tweed jacket and he was frowning down at her.

'Are you in pain?'

'No. Not much. Well, maybe a little heart-sore,' she said with an attempt to smile. 'I'm about to lose Bellbird. But I did know it might be on the cards so…' She shrugged.

He said nothing, then he reached for a cardigan lying over the back of a chair and handed it to her.

Her eyes widened. 'What's this? I'm not cold, not yet, anyway.'

'You could be. We're going out.'

'Where? No, I mean I don't feel like going out.' She regarded him with a frown and said something silly but she was feeling bruised and battered. 'Don't think you can call all the shots, Carlos.'

'Will you stop being tedious, Mia?' he shot back. 'We're going out to dinner whether you like it or not. Why you shouldn't like it is beyond me. You're not up to cooking and I'm still a P-plater when it comes to—'

'A *what*?' she interrupted.

'A pupil when it comes to cooking, like a learner driver.'

'Last night—'

'Oh, I can drive a microwave,' he said with a wave of his hand, 'but I don't happen to feel like anything microwaved tonight. I feel like something hearty, like an inch-thick steak with English mustard hot enough to make my eyes water. Like hot chips, crisp on the outside and soft and fluffy inside, like grilled mushrooms.'

He paused, then continued. 'Maybe a side salad, but not one with all those weird leaves—I'm very conventional when it comes to my salads. I like iceberg lettuce. And when I've finished that I'd like a nice piece of cheese, some cheddar, perhaps, and then something light and sweet but not too sweet, like lemon meringue and not a lot, just a slice followed by real coffee, Kona perhaps, from Hawaii.'

They stared at each other. He was resting his fists on the other side of her desk.

'Oh,' was all Mia could think of to say. But a moment later, 'My mother makes the best lemon meringue.'

He grinned fleetingly. 'The Northern Rivers might be a bit far to go. But we could try Blackheath.' He straightened. 'It's raining again. Would you like me to carry you to the car?'

'No,' she said hastily. 'I mean—' she got up and reached for her crutch, cast a quick upward glance at his expression—and there was a wicked little glint of pure amusement in his eyes, damn him! '—I mean I can manage.'

'Good.' He watched her for a moment more, then turned to lead the way and open the doors.

It was a small, dim little restaurant in Blackheath he took her to but when he asked what she'd like to order she could only stare blindly down at the menu in front of her.

'All right, I'll order for you,' he murmured.

A couple of minutes later she had a glass of golden wine and in due course his steak and a herb omelette for her arrived.

Good choice, she thought with the only part of her brain that seemed to be functioning, *I couldn't have coped with anything heavier.*

In the end she finished the omelette and ate her roll

before she finally sat back and said with a tinge of surprise, 'I didn't know I was hungry.'

He finished his steak.

'How was it?' she queried. 'As mouth-watering as
you described it earlier?'

He grimaced. 'I got a bit carried away, but almost.
So, they're not going to renew the lease?'

'No. My two lovely old ladies have handed over their
affairs, including their enduring power of attorney, and
they've signed Bellbird over as well, to their nephew.'
She fiddled with her napkin. 'And he's decided to put
it on the market.'

'I'm sorry.'

Mia lifted her glass and cupped the bowl of it in the
palm of her hand, the stem between her fingers, as she
watched the liquid swirling around. 'But that's not the
only problem,' she said finally. 'I did have written into
the lease should this happen that I needed at least six
months' notice because I had to be able to take forward
bookings.' She paused. 'Even six months is not very
long; some people have wanted to book from year to
year. Some weddings are planned nine—' she gestured
'—twelve months in advance.'

'So you'll have to cancel some forward bookings
you took over the six months mark?'

She shook her head. 'I didn't take any over the six
months mark, although I have a lot under it. But the
nephew wants to contest the six months' notice.'

Carlos narrowed his eyes. 'Does he have a leg to
stand on?'

Mia sighed. 'I don't know. He's threatened me with

the fact that his aunts may not have been in their right minds when they signed the lease, that I may even have exerted undue influence on them. I think—' Mia twirled her glass and sighed '—I get the feeling he's in financial straits and he really needs to sell Bellbird.'

'*He* may have been the one who exerted undue influence,' Carlos said meditatively.

'I wondered about that, but the thought of going to court...' She shook her head. 'I may not have much choice, though. *I* could get sued for leaving some of the closer functions in the lurch.'

He sat back and placed his napkin on the table. 'Apart from that, are you confident you'll find somewhere else and be able to get a business up and going again?' he asked.

Mia shook her head. 'Not confident. I've got butterflies in my stomach—terrible fears would be more accurate—that I won't be able to, but I'll push on. Somehow.'

He said, as he pushed his plate away, 'Not a great couple of days.'

'No,' she agreed. She rubbed her forehead, then collected her loose hair in one hand and drew it in a thick rope over her shoulder.

'I like your hair loose.'

Mia looked up and their gazes caught and held across the table. And something in the way he was looking at her ignited a rush of awareness in her as well as sending her pulse racing.

Heavens above, she thought, it would be so easy to seek solace and comfort, from a cruel blow on top of everything else, in his arms. It would be not only that but something she craved, she acknowledged, still staring into his eyes and feeling herself drowning in their grey depths.

But she had to break this spell. She made herself look away and blink a couple of times.

'Mia.' He said her name very quietly.

'Tell me more about Nina.'

She bit her lip, then thought, why shouldn't she ask about her?

'I don't know why you're looking like that,' she said evenly.

He raised an eyebrow. 'Like what?'

'As if—' she paused '—as if I'm being ridiculous.'

His lips twisted. 'If I did, it was because I don't see the connection—thank you,' he said to the waitress delivering their coffee.

She blushed and tripped as she walked away.

This time it was Mia who expressed unspoken irony—she looked heavenward.

'We seem to be at cross purposes,' Carlos said lazily, sitting back and looking even more amused.

Mia controlled herself with difficulty. 'You don't see the connection? OK! Let's put it in black and white,' she said tartly. 'You've virtually come straight from Nina French's arms to being—to looking—to...' She stopped helplessly.

'To being possessed of the desire to have and to hold you?' he supplied and sat forward to rest his elbow on the table and his chin on his fist. 'You know, it's a funny thing but that desire seems to exist on its own.

It seems to have a life of its own. It doesn't seem to be susceptible to anything else that's going on all around it—if you know what I mean.'

'I…' Mia stopped, frowned at him, looked away, then looked back as if jerked on a string. 'I'm not sure what you do mean,' she said uncertainly.

'Simple. Since I got clobbered on the head by a falling branch, I only have to be in your company to want you. In my bed, in case there's any misunderstanding. Whatever the other circumstances of my life happen to be.'

Mia was dead still for a long moment, then she clicked her tongue in sheer frustration and stood up, ready to walk away. 'You're impossible! Actually you're crazy, Carlos O'Connor. What you're describing—the way you're describing us makes it sound as if we exist in a bubble. It doesn't sound *real*,' she said intensely.

There was silence for a long moment, then she said quietly, 'That's why I want to know about Nina. And if *she's* real for you.'

He stood up and it stunned her to see that he *was* suddenly grimly serious. 'Nina and I are washed up. I never should have let it go on for so long but my dearest wish is for her to find someone who understands her better than I did. Someone who anchors her and loves her even when the impossible things about her make it…almost impossible to do so.'

Mia blinked several times and sat down.

He stared down at her for a long moment and she was shocked by the harsh lines scored into his face, then he sat down himself.

'I'm sorry,' Mia said quietly but her throat worked. 'I didn't realise it was so painful for you.'

'Painful?' He picked up his glass and studied it. 'I wish to hell I knew what it actually was.'

Mia opened her mouth, then decided to keep her thoughts on that subject to herself. 'Shall we go?' she said tentatively. 'We're the only ones left and they might be wanting to close up. I'll just visit the powder room.'

'Sure.' He signalled for the bill and when she came back he helped her out to the car. It was still raining.

'Damn,' Mia said as they drove along.

He looked questioningly at her.

'I've got a garden club coming for lunch tomorrow. They're really keen to see the Bellbird gardens.'

'It could be a whole new world tomorrow,' he said wryly.

Mia smiled. 'It's what I need. But I doubt there'll be much change, although the sun may shine. By the way, Gail made up two beds in the main house for tonight—'

'Oh,' he interrupted, 'didn't I tell you? I've made different arrangements for tonight. Gail's coming to stay with you after her Girl Guides session ends.'

Mia's mouth fell open. 'No, you didn't tell me. Neither did Gail—she didn't say a word to me. Not about tonight.'

'She didn't know before she left work this afternoon. I didn't get around to making these other arrangements until quite late.' He looked across at her. 'I didn't think you'd mind.'

'I…well…' She stopped helplessly.

'You don't sound too sure and you look cross,' he

observed. 'In light of your extreme agitation on the subject last night, I'm surprised.'

Mia gritted her teeth. 'It's just that I like to know what's going on. When did you get in touch with Gail?'

'While you were in the powder room.'

'You…I…*how* did you get in touch with her?'

'I rang her last night, remember? So I've got her number in my mobile phone. Anything further you'd like to know, Sergeant Gardiner?' He turned into Bellbird's driveway just after, as it happened, Gail did and they followed her tail-lights up the driveway.

'*Why?*'

'I've decided to go back to Sydney tonight—hell, I forgot about Long John. I'll drive down—'

'You don't have to,' Mia said.

'But you can't let him starve. That could make him worse than ever.'

'He won't starve—I've given him to someone to look after.'

'Someone he won't bite, I hope, but how do you know he won't bite *this* person?'

'Because *this* person bit him back,' Mia replied and dissolved into laughter. 'I'm sorry,' she said finally, still giggling, 'I think it's all been a bit much for me but it does have its funny side. And don't you dare carry me out of this car and inside. I can manage. Take care in Sydney.' She patted his arm, and struggled out with her crutch.

'What's so funny?' Gail asked as they met at the front door. 'Are you laughing or crying?'

'I don't know.' Mia rubbed her face. 'Well, yes, I do. You were right—it's much cosier down at the cottage, Gail, so shall we go down there and start a fire and have a drink? As someone once said, what's the point in being sober *and* virtuous at this end of the day?'

'Who said that? Shakespeare?'

'No—just someone I know.' Mia climbed into Gail's car and stowed her crutch. 'Not that I'm unsober. I've only had one glass of wine. Mind you, now I come to think of it, maybe I don't have anything to drink after last night.'

'Just as well it's me.' Gail climbed into the driver's side and she hauled a bottle of wine out of her bag. 'Don't know why but I thought to pop this in with my PJs.'

'Gail, you're a treasure.' Mia leant over to kiss her assistant on the cheek. 'You wouldn't believe the kind of day I've had. Or the last couple of hours, anyway. Oh, Gail, I've got some bad news.'

'Wait,' Gail advised as she drove down the track to the cottage. 'I know a bit of it, anyway.'

'How? Don't tell me Carlos told you!'

Gail nodded. 'He said you could be feeling a bit delicate so I was to take care of you on his behalf till he gets back.'

Mia stared at Gail in the gloom of the car. 'He said that?'

'Yep.' Gail coasted to a stop, switched off and doused the lights.

'He takes a lot upon himself,' Mia said indistinctly, in the grip of an emotion she found hard to name—

anger at his high-handed ways? Helplessness? Or the faintest whisper like a tiny echo in her heart that told her how wonderful it would be to have Carlos to turn to, for advice, for mental support? To help her to shore up her shaken defences?

'If I had Carlos O'Connor on my side,' Gail said with a certain militancy but almost as if she'd read Mia's mind, 'and thinking of me, I'd be a bit more gracious about it than you are, Mia. Now, will you come in and get warm and maybe a bit unsober?'

CHAPTER FOUR

THE SUN CHOSE to shine on the garden club lunch the next day and Gail, with the help of her sister Kylie, managed brilliantly.

Mia spent most of the day sitting in her office talking on the phone and working on the computer. She'd tossed and turned all night under the twin weights of losing Bellbird and what she thought of as the irrefutable knowledge that Carlos was still in love with Nina, much as he might wish otherwise.

Trying to seek legal advice as well as trying to find a venue she could transfer functions to did not do anything to cheer her up.

She had another twenty-four hours before she had to make a response to Bellbird's new owner but she couldn't make up her mind whether to go to court or not.

Finally, late afternoon, when all the guests had left, the clear air lured her out into the garden. She hopped over to a bench and sank down. The sunlight was warm on her skin; she was wearing a soft green summer dress that matched her eyes. And, because she'd not been on show, her hair was only lightly tied back.

The gardens were beautiful. The rain had freshened them up, there were bees and dragonflies hovering over the flowers, there were delicate scents on the air, there was the unique aura of Mount Wilson, and there were bellbirds calling.

Don't cry, she warned herself as she closed her eyes and gave herself over to the magic of the estate.

It was the roar of Carlos's car that roused her from her reverie.

She opened her eyes and watched it pull up at the main house. She saw Carlos get out and stretch, then walk inside.

Carlos, she thought with a sudden pang as well as an accelerated heartbeat. Despite all her own catastrophes, she'd not only tossed and turned overnight, she'd had Carlos and Nina French at the back of her mind all day.

It had sounded—from what he'd said last night— as if they couldn't live together but they couldn't live without each other. It had sounded like a relationship fraught with tearing, deep emotion, like a battlefield, but she got the feeling that while those tearing emotions might hurt deeply, the other side of the coin could be heights such as they'd never known with anyone else.

But, whatever it was, in comparison, her own romantic dealings with Carlos had sounded trivial.

She had to forget about him. He never was for her and he never would be.

It was the clink of glass that drew her out of her reverie this time and she opened her eyes again to see Carlos crossing the lawn towards her with a tray bearing a jug and a couple of glasses.

He was wearing jeans, boots and a blue-and-white striped shirt with the neck open and the sleeves rolled up. He looked impossibly attractive with his dark hair and olive skin, with his height and wide shoulders, his lean body...

'Hi!' she said, taking a very deep breath. 'Welcome back, but if that's alcohol I think I should abstain.'

He grinned. 'Gail told me you and she demolished a bottle of wine last night. No, it's fresh fruit juice, not at all spiked.'

He put the tray down on a wrought iron table and sat down next to her on the bench. 'How's the foot?'

'Not bad. I'm getting the hang of the crutches now—there's a bit of an art to it. I—' she hesitated '—I wasn't sure if you were coming back. You didn't need to. I'm being very well looked after.'

'Good.'

'Thank you all the same—' she interrupted '—for all your help. I don't want to seem ungracious.'

'Ungracious?' He looked quizzical.

'That's what Gail said I was.' She bit her lip.

'So Gail's giving you lessons in tact and diplomacy?' he hazarded. 'Should be interesting.'

Mia regarded him for a long moment with an expression of deep hostility. 'Between the two of you,' she said bitterly, 'it's not surprising I'm feeling like a nervous wreck. *I am not ungrateful for your help*, Carlos,' she said, emphasising each word. 'That's all I'm trying to say.'

'Good,' he replied comfortably and handed her a glass of fruit juice. 'Lovely out here, isn't it?' He looked around.

'Yes,' she said on a little sigh. 'Hear the bellbirds?'

He listened. 'Yes. How was your day?'

Mia sighed. 'Pretty disheartening. I haven't come up with an alternative yet and I can't make up my mind whether to go to court or not, but—' she gestured and squared her shoulders '—tomorrow's another day—I think it was Scarlett O'Hara who said something like that.'

'No doubt after Rhett told her he couldn't give a damn.' He looked amused. 'Uh...I have some better news for you. I've bought it.'

'Bought what?' she asked automatically.

'This place.' He waved a hand.

Mia choked. Even the bellbirds seemed to stop calling in the long moments before she could gather her wits to reply. Then she turned to him, her face suddenly pale, her eyes huge, dark and uncomprehending.

'What do you mean? What are you talking about?'

He put his hand along the back of the bench behind her. 'I bought Bellbird,' he said slowly and precisely.

'*Bought it*?' she echoed huskily, still looking stunned. 'Why?'

He withdrew his arm and sat forward with his hands between his knees. 'So you can stay on. You can lease it from me for as long as you want. But there were other reasons. I had this vision planted in my mind of a girl in a long white dress, carrying a big hat and playing ladies on a hill station. A girl with heavy, midnight-dark hair and green eyes. Wait,' he murmured as Mia stirred. 'Let me finish.'

He thought for a moment. 'A girl I admired and—'

'And felt sorry for,' Mia said out of a clogged throat. 'Please don't go on.'

He put a hand on her knee. 'No, I don't feel sorry for you, Mia. There's something about you that doesn't go with sickly sentimental stuff like that. But I do like to repay my debts.'

'You don't owe me anything.'

'Yes, I do,' he countered. 'Between myself and my mother, we must have created hell for you. I also—' he paused '—need to apologise for the possibly flippant way I described the effect you have on me from time to time.'

Mia blinked.

'Not that it doesn't happen,' he added dryly. 'But you're right, there's something a bit unreal about it.'

Mia flinched inwardly and immediately called herself a fool. Why did it hurt? She'd told herself only hours ago he wasn't the one for her; he'd never been. And her beleaguered mind turned to the fact that he'd bought Bellbird.

'I can't believe you bought it,' she said shakily.

He shrugged. 'It's a little bit of heaven. Who wouldn't want it if they could have it? Besides—' all of a sudden he sounded cold and grim '—there's not a lot I can do about a nephew exerting undue pressure on his elderly aunts but the details of the sale include me taking over your lease and deducting a compensatory amount from the sale price.'

Mia blinked. 'I don't know what to say. I wish you hadn't.' It was a sentiment that slipped out unexpectedly but it was true, she realised. Despite everything she felt for the property and her business, she wished he hadn't.

'Why?'

She interlaced her fingers. 'It makes me feel beholden to you.'

He swore beneath his breath.

She hesitated and in the grip of a maelstrom of emotions, she rubbed her face distractedly. 'It also puts me in an impossible position.'

'What does?' There was a distinct coolness in his voice now.

Mia put a hand to her mouth. 'To think you bought Bellbird because of me and therefore I should, out of gratitude, do anything you want.'

'Perish the thought,' he said harshly. 'You don't really believe I'm going to blackmail you into anything, do you?'

She was silent.

'But—' he paused '—if you didn't want to stay, you could have your six months to get you out of any contractual difficulties and then—' he grimaced, folded his arms across his chest and stretched his legs out '—we would come to our final parting of the ways, Mia, at least with me knowing I'd done as much as I was allowed to, to compensate for what happened seven years ago.'

Mia jumped up, her eyes flashing, and fell over as her injured heel hit the ground.

Carlos was on his feet immediately and he picked her up and held her in his arms as she struggled.

'Whoa!' he admonished. 'What the hell do you think I'm going to do? Here.' He handed her the crutch and put his hands on her hips until she steadied.

Then, to her fury, he tidied her hair with his hands and pushed it back over one shoulder. 'I see what you mean about the crutch,' he said as he straightened the collar of her dress. 'Not only are you one-legged but you're one-handed—awkward.'

Mia breathed deeply and Carlos sat down again and drained his glass.

'Go on, I'm all ears,' he drawled.

'Look, please don't think I'm not grateful—'

'Here we go again,' he murmured. 'You're a good teacher, Gail.'

'All *right*,' she said through her teeth with sudden tears streaming down her face. 'I will *never* forgive your mother for what she did, how she made me feel. I will never forgive *you*—' she broke off and realised that it might have come seven years late but it was true '—for not checking up on me, even if it had been to come and say, "Mia, I *could only mess up your life*."'

'Mia—'

But she waved him to silence. 'Nor will I ever forgive your mother for coming back into my life and patronising me all over again. This—' she gestured to take in Bellbird '—can't change that and if I did stay

on I'd feel terrible because I'd still feel the same way.
Don't you see?'

'All right.' He stood up and put the glasses back on
the tray. 'But you'd be well advised to stay for the six
months. Protracted legal dealings can cost a fortune.
Don't worry.' He looked down at her sardonically. 'I
won't trouble you at all.'

Mia discovered she was trembling all over and she
still had tears rolling down her cheeks. 'Look, I'm sorry
if I…if…'

'Forget it,' he said. 'Better to know where we stand.
You hold your crutch.'

Mia looked up at him. 'What do you mean?'

'This, no doubt for the last time, Mia.' And he picked
her up effortlessly and started to stride across the lawn
with her.

Mia was struck dumb because, apart from kissing
her, he couldn't have done anything that affected her
senses more drastically. To feel herself cradled against
his hard, toned body, to inhale that tantalising smell of
sweat and fresh cotton sent ripples of desire and need
through her.

Then he compounded it as they reached the house.

He set her carefully on her feet, waited until she
was steady on her crutch, then he kissed her full on the
mouth with his hand cupping her head.

'Take care, Miss Firebrand,' he advised with an
ironic little glint in his eye. 'Take care.'

He made sure she was steady again and walked away
to his car.

It was Gail who came out to stand beside Mia as Carlos accelerated down the drive. It was Gail who put her arm around Mia's shaking shoulders and led her inside.

CHAPTER FIVE

SIX WEEKS LATER Mia put down the phone and stared into space, her mind reeling.

She was still at Bellbird, having, after serious thought and some legal advice, written Carlos a stilted little note to the effect that she would be grateful to stay on for the six-month term of her original lease. She'd got a reply agreeing to her request, written and signed by his secretary.

Gail happened to be passing the office doorway with a pile of snowy tablecloths in her arms but she paused and raised an interrogative eyebrow at her boss.

'That was Carol Manning,' Mia said in a preoccupied manner.

Gail waited a moment, then, 'Do I know Carol Manning?'

'Uh…no, sorry.' Mia tapped her teeth with her pencil. 'She's Carlos O'Connor's secretary.'

Gail advanced into the office and dumped the tablecloths on a chair. 'What's he want?'

'A lunch for forty next week. They're holding some kind of a conference on the two preceding days and have decided to wrap things up with a lunch.'

'Not a great deal of notice,' Gail observed. 'He's lucky you had the day free.'

'He...' Mia paused. 'He had something else planned, a cruise on the harbour, but the long range forecast is for showers and high winds now—in Sydney, that is, it's only a coastal low pressure system, apparently. It should be OK up here. I can't help wondering why he didn't choose another venue, though.'

Gail grimaced. 'Why should he when he owns the best venue there is?'

Mia smiled dryly. 'In a nutshell,' she murmured. 'I still wish he'd gone somewhere else.'

'I can understand that.' Gail picked up her table-cloths. 'Considering the way things ended between you two. Not that I've asked any questions, but you only had to have eyes.'

'Gail, you've been a tower of strength and I really appreciate the fact that you haven't asked any questions,' Mia said warmly. 'I just...I'm just not sure how I'll be.'

'You'll be fine! At least you can walk on two feet now. OK—' she dumped the tablecloths on a chair again and sat down opposite Mia '—let's help you to be fine; let's slay 'em. Let's give them the best darn lunch they've ever had. Is there any kind of theme to the conference—did this Carol Manning mention anything pivotal?'

'Horses,' Mia said succinctly. 'O'Connor Construction is planning to build an equestrian centre that should accommodate stabling, tracks for thoroughbreds, tracks for trotters, dressage plus a vet hospital, swimming pools for horses, you name it. Thus, at the conference there'll be a variety of people from vets to trainers to owners to jockeys, but all horsey.'

'I'm quite a fan of horses,' Gail observed, looking thoughtful.

'I am too.' Mia chewed the end of her pencil this time. 'Gail, you're a genius. I've just had the most amazing idea.'

'I don't see how that makes *me* a genius.'

'It was your "pivotal" point that did it. You may not know it, but one of the most famous horse races in the world is the Kentucky Derby.'

'Well, I did know that.'

'Good.' Mia turned to her computer and her fingers flew over the keys as she did some research. 'The other thing about it is the fact that it's laden with tradition. You drink mint juleps at Churchill Downs on Kentucky Derby day, you eat burgoo—'

'I've heard of mint juleps but what on earth is burgoo?'

'It's a concoction of beef, chicken, pork and vegetables,' Mia read from her screen, 'and they play Stephen Foster's "My Old Kentucky Home" while you do. Then there are the roses.'

'We've got plenty of roses,' Gail put in.

'I know.' Mia thought of the rose gardens outside in full bloom. 'The tradition is that the winner, the horse, is draped in a blanket woven with five hundred and fifty-four roses. We probably—' she looked up at Gail '—don't have to use that many roses, then again we do need a horse.'

'Not a live one. Certainly not Long John—he could go about biting all manner of people,' Gail objected.

'Nooo—but I can't think what else to substitute. Apart from that, though, wouldn't it be something to serve a horsey crowd mint juleps and—' she pointed to her screen '—feed them burgoo from an authentic recipe—and have the waiters and waitresses dressed in jockey silks?'

Gail blinked. 'The mint juleps sound a bit dangerous if you ask me.'

'The guests are coming by coach so we don't need to worry about drink-driving. A horse, a horse,' Mia said rapidly, 'my kingdom for a horse.'

'My mother's got one; it's a wooden rocking horse, it's nearly as big as the real thing and it's in beautiful condition for an antique. It's Mum's pride and joy.'

'Oh, Gail, do you think she'd lend it to us?'

'We can only ask. What else do we need?'

'Stephen Foster music, but I'm sure I can find that. All right.' Mia sat up. 'I won't have time to think straight.'

'Five hundred and fifty-four roses?' Bill James said incredulously. 'You must be mad, Mia. Clean off your rocker, more like it.'

'If you'd let me finish, Bill,' Mia said with a slight edge, 'I was just telling you that's the number they use in the actual Kentucky Derby to decorate the winner's blanket.'

'They, whoever they are, sound as nutty as fruitcakes

too, if you ask me,' Bill interjected. 'Five hundred and fifty-four. For a horse blanket!'

'Bill—' Mia breathed heavily '—we won't use *nearly* as many but we will use *some*—so be prepared.' She eyed him militantly.

Bill snorted and then eyed *her*. 'You're getting snippety, Mia. Not only that, you're looking peaky. If I were you, I'd get that boyfriend of yours back.'

Mia went to speak but choked instead and finally turned on her heel, the good one, and marched away.

To her dismay, she found herself tossing and turning in her loft the night before the O'Connor lunch, despite her earlier conviction that, with the forthcoming event to think about, she would be too busy to think of anything else.

Finally she got up, climbed down her ladder, put some more wood into the stove and brewed herself a cup of chocolate.

In the six weeks since she'd last seen Carlos, she'd had days when she was sure, quite convinced, in fact, that she'd done the right thing. Even accepting the six months had gone against the grain with her. It had made her feel like the recipient of charity. It made her, as unreasonable as it sounded, but she couldn't help it, feel like the housekeeper's daughter again.

But on other days she thought she must have been a little mad to have knocked back the opportunity to stay on at Bellbird.

Why couldn't she have buried her pride? After all, it had been her dream only a few weeks ago. Even now, as she resolutely looked for new premises to move to when her lease was up, it was tearing her apart to think of leaving.

But that's nonsense, she thought as she sipped her chocolate. It's only a place.

And he's only a man, but like it or not I've had a crush on Carlos for a long time, and probably always will….

She stared into the fire and shivered, not from cold, but from fear. She was feeling scared and young because she was confused, because she was sometimes tempted to think she could love Carlos much better than Nina French had.

In fact loving Carlos, or the thought of it, was something that plagued her waking hours as well as her dreams.

It was mad. No sooner had she told him she could never forgive him, no sooner had she told him she wished he hadn't bought Bellbird, than she'd started to feel bereft and in a particular way.

She missed him. She shook secretly with desire for him. She missed the way he charmed people, like Gail's mother. She desperately missed the way he forked back his hair, how his eyes could laugh at her while his expression was grave. The feel of him when he carried her in his arms…

The next morning Mia dressed carefully in a skirt and blouse.

She'd tied her hair back but used a lilac scarf to lessen the severity of the style.

Then, having checked with the caterers that everything was going well with the 'burgoo'—she gave it a taste test—she took a last tour of the dining room.

Pride of place on a dais was Gail's mother's rocking horse, looking spectacular under its 'rose blanket', which was a work of art, even if nothing like five hundred and fifty-four roses had been used. And in the centre of the room there was an ice carving of a mare with her foal at her foot.

'My Old Kentucky Home' was playing softly in the background and waitresses in jockey silks and caps were waiting to serve mint juleps.

Then the guests arrived and Mia held her breath as they filtered into the dining room but she was reassured by the gasps and delighted comments, and she sought out Gail across the room with her eyes and they gave each other the thumbs-up sign.

There was no sign of Carlos, although Carol Manning had introduced herself. 'He should be here any minute,' she said with some obvious frustration. 'He's often late.'

'I know, he was late for his sister's wedding,' Mia said and bit her lip. 'Uh…he didn't come by bus?'

'Bus! When you have the kind of car he drives, no,' Carol Manning responded and looked more closely at Mia. 'So you're Mia Gardiner? How do you do? I must say—' she looked around, wide-eyed '—I can understand why Mr O'Connor decided to have you do this lunch. It's inspired. Ah, here he is now.' And she nodded to the entrance of the dining room.

Carlos was standing in the doorway, looking around.

He wore a beautifully tailored grey suit, a pale blue shirt and a navy tie. Then, with a faint smile twisting his lips, he came across the room and, for an instant, Mia felt like fainting under the almost overpowering impact of his good looks, his masculinity and what he used to mean to her.

'Well done, Miss Gardiner,' he said. 'Very well done. How's the foot?'

'Fine now, thank you, Mr O'Connor,' she murmured. 'I'll leave you to it. Enjoy your lunch.' And she moved away smoothly.

'So here you are.'

Mia looked up with a start. She was in her cottage having seen, or so she thought, the last of the lunch guests off.

It had clearly been a highly successful function. Carlos had been nowhere to be seen, nor had his car.

'I thought you'd gone,' she said.

'Or hoped I had? Never mind. I actually went to see Gail's mother.' He sat down at the kitchen table.

'What on earth for?' Mia frowned.

'Gail told me she wove the rose blanket so I went to thank her.'

'That was nice,' Mia conceded.

'You sound surprised.'

'No, I've always known you can be nice.' Mia said flatly, then added on a rush of breath, 'What do you want, Carlos? We've got nothing more to say to each other.'

He raised an eyebrow. 'You may not have but it looks

to me as if you've lost weight. Finding it a bit hard to maintain a stance so full of righteous indignation, Mia?'

She gasped. 'How dare you? It's not that!'

'Then what is it?'

'I mean, I haven't lost weight,' she corrected herself belatedly, but it was a lie. She was not prepared to admit as much to Carlos, however.

'According to Bill, not only don't you look well but you're cranky and hard to work with.'

Mia opened her mouth, closed it, then, 'Hard to work with?' she repeated furiously. 'If anyone is hard to work with it's Bill. Have you any idea how I have to nurse him through Lucy's month with her grandkids?' She broke off, breathing heavily.

He watched the way her chest heaved beneath the black blouse, then looked into her eyes. 'If it's any comfort,' he said quietly, 'I'm like a bear with a sore head at times too.'

Her lips parted. 'Why?' she whispered.

'Whatever the rights and wrongs of it, I want you. I thought you might be in the same difficulty.'

She was transfixed as she turned pale then pink in a way that virtually shouted from the rooftops that she was.

'I…I…' she stammered and couldn't go on.

He moved a step closer but that was when her phone rang. It was lying on the kitchen table and she was all set to ignore it but she saw her mother's name on the screen and picked it up to answer.

Her tears were impossible to control when she ended the call and she was white to the lips.

'What?' he asked. 'What's happened?'

'My father. He's had a stroke. Oh, I've got to go but it could take me hours to get off the mountain, let alone up to Ballina.' She wrung her hands.

'No, it won't.' He pulled his own phone out and punched in some numbers.

Half an hour later Mia was on her way down the mountain beside him in his fast car and when they reached Sydney Airport she transferred to a waiting helicopter he'd organised.

'There'll be a car at the airport to take you to the hospital,' he told her just before she boarded the chopper.

'I can't thank you enough!'

'Don't worry about it,' he recommended.

She turned away to climb aboard, then turned back impulsively and kissed him swiftly. 'Thanks,' she said from the bottom of her heart.

A week later her father, who'd been moved to the Lismore Base Hospital, was recovering.

It was going to take some months of physiotherapy for him to be as mobile as he had been, but all the signs were good. And her mother had returned from the shell-shocked, frightened, trembling person she'd been at first to her usual practical and positive self.

'I think we'll lease the tea room out,' she'd told Mia. 'You know, apart from the birds and the bees and growing things, your father has always had another ambition—to drive around Australia. I think the time has come, when he's recovered, to buy a caravan and do it.'

'Why not?' Mia had responded.

Her mother had then looked at her critically and told her she looked as if she needed a break.

Mia agreed with her but didn't tell her she actually felt as if she'd been run over by a bus. Instead she mentioned that she planned to have a couple of days off before she returned to Mount Wilson, since Gail seemed to be coping well and now had Lucy James to help her out.

Mia's mother had looked unconvinced about the efficacy of 'a couple of days' but she'd urged Mia just to do it.

Mia took herself to Byron Bay, south of the Queensland border and the most easterly point of the Australian mainland.

She booked herself into a luxury motel just across the road from the beach and she slept for hours on her first day.

Then she took a stroll down the beach at sunset.

It was a beautiful scene, a pink cloud-streaked sky, the sheen of pewter laid across the placid low-tide water and the lighthouse an iridescent white on the dark green of Cape Byron.

She rolled her jeans up and splashed in the shallows. Her hair was loose and wild. She had a turquoise T-shirt on and she'd tied a beige jumper round her waist by its sleeves. On her way back she stopped to untie it and pull it on as the pink of the sunset slipped from the sky and the air cooled.

That was when she noticed a tall figure standing on the beach below the surf club.

A tall figure she could never mistake—Carlos.

She didn't hesitate. She pushed her arms into the sleeves of the jumper as she walked over to him.

'I didn't know you were here, Carlos.'

'I wasn't. I've only just arrived. Your mother told me you were here.'

'Oh, Carlos! You spoke to my mother?'

He nodded. 'And your father. I went to see them.'

'They would have loved that. Thanks a million. Where are you staying?'

He took her hand and touched the side of her face, then pushed her hair behind her ears. 'With you, Mia. With you if you'll have me.'

She took a breath and a faint smile curved her lips. 'Just as well it's only across the road then,' she said serenely.

'I like the way you do that,' Mia murmured.

She was lying naked across the king-sized bed and her body was afire with his touch as he left no part of her unexplored.

'But I think I need to be held before I…I don't know what, but something tempestuous is liable to happen to me, Carlos,' she went on with a distinct wobble in her voice.

He laughed a little wickedly and took her in his arms. 'How's that?'

'Oh, thanks.' She wound her arms round him and kissed the strong tanned column of his neck. 'You know, I can't believe this.'

'Believe what?' He cupped her bottom.

'How good it is to be here in bed with you,' she said on a genuine note of wonderment. She leant up on one elbow and looked at him seriously. 'It's not too tame for you, is it?'

'Tame?' he replied equally as seriously and removed his hands from her hips to cup her breasts. Her nipples hardened as he played with them and she took several ragged little breaths.

He looked into her eyes. 'Tame?' he repeated as she writhed against him and bit her bottom lip. 'It's the opposite, but are you ready for me, Mia?'

'More than that, dying, actually. Oh!' she gasped as he turned her onto her back and eased his body onto hers. And she was ready to welcome him so that in moments the rhythm of their lovemaking increased and there was absolutely nothing tame about the way they moved together and finally climaxed together—it was wild, wanton and wonderful.

In fact Mia couldn't speak for a few minutes afterwards as she lay cradled in his arms, her body slick with sweat, her hair a cloud of rough black silk on the pillow. And she made a tiny sound when he moved—a sound of protest.

'It's OK,' he reassured her and pulled the sheet up. 'I'm going nowhere.'

She relaxed.

Mia sat cross-legged on the beach early the next morning, sifting sand through her fingers as she watched Carlos body-surfing into the beach.

She'd given up on her hair and hadn't even bothered to pin it back. She wore short white shorts and her turquoise T-shirt, she was barefoot and, because of a playful breeze, she'd pulled on Carlos's sweatshirt.

It was miles too big for her but it not only made her feel warm, it was like having his arms around her.

She was smiling at absolutely nothing at all.

'Hi.' He stood in front of her, droplets of water still sliding down his sleek tanned body, and picked up his towel as he studied her dimples. 'Something funny?'

'No,' she assured him. 'Oh, you'll want your top.' She started to take his sweatshirt off.

'Keep it on,' he said. 'I'll use the towel—now you're laughing!' He looked around. 'What is it?' He sat down beside her.

'It's me,' she told him.

He grimaced. 'What's so funny about you?'

'You know those stereotyped women you see on TV and in the movies who float around radiantly on cloud nine after someone has made love to them?'

'Uh-huh.' He rubbed his hair with the towel and looked at her quizzically. 'Not...?' He didn't finish.

'Yep.' She nodded vigorously. 'That's who I remind myself of this morning. Or those smiley faces on computers.'

'The smiley trail?' He started to laugh and pulled her into his arms and lay back on the sand with her. 'You're crazy,' he teased.

'And you're wonderful,' she replied, sobering. 'There is something else your lovemaking has achieved, though.'

'I hesitate to ask,' he said ruefully.

'I could eat a horse,' she told him. 'I'm *starving.*'

'Ah—' he sat up with her still in his arms '—now there we are of the same mind. Let's go.'

They got back to their room and Mia showered while Carlos ordered breakfast.

When she emerged, breakfast had not arrived but a bottle of champagne stood in an ice bucket on the coffee table next to two flutes and a flask of orange juice.

'Oh,' she said, recalling their conversation about morning-after champagne celebrations. 'Dangerous and delightful.'

Carlos had showered at the beach and he wore khaki shorts and a white shirt. His hair was still damp and hanging in his eyes. His feet were bare but he was enough to make her heart beat faster and then, when he came and ran his hands down her body, over her colourful cotton sarong, all the fire he'd aroused in her the night before came back to her and she trembled and put her arms around his waist and laid her head on his chest.

'You shouldn't,' she said huskily.

He traced his fingers down the side of her neck and cupped the smooth curve of her shoulder. 'Shouldn't?' He said it barely audibly.

'Touch me. It sets off all sorts of chain reactions.'

She felt his slight jolt of laughter and he kissed the top of her head. 'You're not alone.'

There was a knock on the door.

They drew apart, both laughing.

* * *

It was a glorious day.

She spoke at length to her parents, then they drove up to the lighthouse after lunch and were rewarded as they gazed down at the wrinkled blue ocean to see a pod of humpback whales making their way back to the Southern Ocean after their sojourn in the tropical waters of Queensland.

'There's something about them that always makes me feel emotional,' she said of the whales as they sat on a bench from where they could see not only the ocean to the east of Cape Byron but the protected beaches to the west as well as Mount Warning, and Julian Rocks out in the bay.

'I think it's because they're so big and it's such an amazing journey.' He put his arm around her shoulders. 'Don't cry.'

She sniffed. 'I'm not crying, not really.'

'How about—' he stretched out his legs '—we go out for dinner tonight?'

'Uh…we could. Any special reason?'

He meditated for a moment. 'There's a band playing at the restaurant next door to the motel,' he said, 'so we could eat and dance.'

'Sounds good.'

'But I have an ulterior motive,' he went on. 'I think I would like to see a really glamorous version of you, all dressed and tizzied up, and be confident in the knowledge that when I got you back to our room I'd be able to undo it all.'

Mia choked. 'That's…diabolical.'

He took his arm from her shoulders and sat forward, taking her hand. 'You'd enjoy it, I promise.'

'I…possibly,' she conceded. 'Always assuming I could sit still and eat my dinner with that on my mind. However—' she paused dramatically '—there's one problem.'

He raised an eyebrow at her.

'I didn't bring any smart clothes with me.'

'Ah. Well, look, while I make some calls, why don't you undertake some retail therapy?'

Mia pursed her lips. 'You really think I should?'

'I really do. I've discovered that next to sex—and sometimes even over and above sex—retail therapy does wonders for girls.'

Mia almost went cross-eyed as she struggled not to make a thoroughly exasperated feminist retort to this.

'You don't agree?' he asked.

Mia looked at him. He was still in his khaki shorts and white shirt. The breeze was lifting his hair and the fine white cotton of his shirt.

He looked big, utterly relaxed and sinfully attractive with one dark eyebrow raised quizzically at her. As if he knew exactly what was going through her mind….

She shrugged. 'I don't mind a bit of retail therapy.' She waited for a moment but he said nothing. 'And of course Byron is not a bad spot for it,' she added.

'Bravo!'

Mia blinked. 'What for?'

'Not responding to the bait,' he drawled and put his arms around her.

Mia frowned, squinted, then gave way to laughter. 'How could I? Nothing on earth is going to stop me from going shopping now!'

He kissed her and they got up and strolled back to the car, hand in hand.

Byron Bay, with its village atmosphere and plethora of boutiques and restaurants, was a charming place for a spot of retail therapy.

It was in a glamorous little boutique that Mia found the dress. Chalk-blue in a crinkly fabric, the bodice was sleeveless and moulded to her figure, with tantalising cut-outs from under the arms to the waist. The skirt billowed down her legs with a long slit up one side. A pair of high blue suede sandals could have been made for the outfit so she bought them too.

Then she found a hairdresser and not only had her hair done but her finger and toenails painted a dark blue. It was the hairdresser who directed her to a lingerie shop where she purchased a pair of divine high-cut panties in blue satin and lace. The dress, on account of its cut-outs, had a built-in bra, but, because she was really on a roll, she also bought a sleek ivory silk nightgown that came with a black silk kimono embroidered with ivory birds of paradise that she fell in love with.

She took herself back to the motel, deeply satisfied with her session of 'retail therapy' but wondering how she was going to hide a certain glint in her eye from Carlos. Then she decided she didn't care. She was quite happy to share her euphoria with him.

He wasn't there.

There was a note on the table to the effect that he'd got a call from a business associate who'd found out they were both in Byron, and he'd gone to meet him for a drink. He was, the note said, ready for dinner and he'd meet her at the restaurant next door to the motel.

'It'll give you the time and privacy to do your own thing,' the note finished.

She stared at it and discovered she didn't want the time and privacy to do her own thing. She wanted nothing more than to sit down with him, maybe share a glass of champagne with him, and talk.

Yes, and show him her purchases, perhaps even model them for him, but anyway, she didn't want to be alone.

She dropped her carrier bags on the bed and sat down on it with a sudden sigh. So much to think about; when had this happened? How had she let it happen without any trace of a fight? Why did she hear something like warning bells ringing in her brain?

CHAPTER SIX

SHE WAS READY on the dot of seven.

She was not a hundred per cent happy about walking the short distance to the restaurant on her own. Not that she was afraid of being mugged or anything like that; she suddenly felt more dressed up than most people would be, an out of place sort of feeling. She turned to the kitchenette to pour herself a glass of water but a sound from the sliding glass door that led out to the garden and the pool arrested her, and she swung back on her beautiful new heels.

It was Carlos.

He wore a dark suit, a pale shirt and a navy tie.

He looked completely serious, even inscrutably so in a way that highlighted his dark looks.

And they stayed poised like that for what seemed like an eternity, staring at each other across the wide expanse of the bed.

It was an extraordinary moment for Mia. Not only the furnishings, the painting of orchids on the wall, the fall of the curtains seemed to be imprinted on her consciousness, but everything about Carlos too.

How wide his shoulders looked beneath the suit—
how different he looked in a suit, come to that, she
thought. Far more impressive than his father ever had.

But, at the same time, it registered with her that there
was an air of mystery about him. As if he was a man she
only knew a small part of, and she shivered suddenly.

He stirred at last and put out a hand.

She hesitated for a moment, then walked forward
to take it.

'You look sensational,' he said barely audibly as the
beautiful dress settled around her legs.

She moistened her lips. 'So do you.'

'I came to get you.'

'I'm glad you did.'

'So am I.' He pulled her a touch closer. 'Someone
on a white horse with wings could have whisked you
up and away over oceans and continents.'

A smile trembled on her lips.

He raised an eyebrow at her. 'Is that what you were
worried about?'

'Hardly,' she murmured. She looked down at herself.
'I felt a little out of place. And maybe a bit shy about
walking into a restaurant on my own. So that's why
I'm glad you came.'

'Good.' He drew her even closer then, right into his
arms. 'Am I allowed to kiss you?'

'That depends.' She brought her hands up against
his chest.

'On what?' he drawled.

'If it's a gentle salutation you have in mind, that's
permitted. I—'

But he interrupted her and bent her backwards over his arm with his other arm around her hips. 'How about this?'

Mia maintained her decorum with an effort. 'If you don't wreck my hair and my make-up, it's fine. If you do—'

'You'll never speak to me again? You'll scream blue murder?' he suggested with a wicked glint.

'No, I'll get changed and go for a jog along the beach. And I'll buy a hamburger for dinner.'

Surprise saw Carlos O'Connor straighten and Mia started to laugh.

'Is that what you really want to do?' he asked, looking startled.

'After all this?' She pushed herself a little away from him and gestured down her figure expressively. 'I wasn't really serious.'

His lips twisted. 'It would be fun, though. We could take a blanket. We could take some wine. It's a full moon tonight. It's mid-week, it's not school holidays, so there aren't many people on the beach and, anyway, I know of a secluded spot.'

Mia put her hands on her hips. 'You...are serious?'

He leant back against the door and folded his arms. '*You* were the one who brought it up.'

'I know, but—' she looked down at herself again '—all this!'

'You could wear it tomorrow night.' He straightened. 'We could just reverse things.'

'Are we staying another night, though? I didn't...I mean, I didn't know.' She broke off.

'I believe Gail is coping brilliantly,' he remarked, 'so why not?'

Mia shrugged. 'You're right. So much for believing I was indispensable.'

'How about it, then?'

She looked up at him. 'Why not? So long as you promise not to seduce me to some other venue tomorrow.'

'I promise we can dress up all over again tomorrow night.'

'Thank you.'

'This is rather lovely,' Mia pronounced as she snuggled up against Carlos in the depression they'd scooped in the sand against a bank and lined with a car rug he kept stored in the boot of his car.

They'd finished hamburgers with the lot: lettuce—iceberg specially requested—pineapple, beetroot, tomato, onion and cheese. There had also been chips. They'd bought a bottle of wine and some plastic glasses to drink it from.

The moon had cleared Cape Byron and was sending down a white light on the sea, and the stars looked within reach.

They were both dressed warmly against the night air.

'Be nice to put all this in a bottle,' she said suddenly.

'We wouldn't need to if we got married. We could do it time and again.'

Mia took an unexpected breath and tensed. 'Carlos, I don't know what to say.'

He picked up her hand and threaded his fingers

through hers. 'Look, it's a thought. What else did you have in mind? An affair?'

'If…I hadn't thought that far ahead. I don't really know what to think. It happened—' she pulled her hand free and gestured a little helplessly '—so out of the blue.'

'Really?' he said with an audible tinge of scepticism.

Mia bit her lip. She sat up suddenly and rested her chin on her knees. 'Maybe not,' she conceded, and paused as she suddenly recalled the horribly embarrassing fact that he'd known about her crush on him.

She grimaced. 'Look, all right, there was always some attraction but—' she hesitated, then said bleakly and honestly '—I've taken a bit of a battering lately.'

'You're not operating on full power, full mental capacity?' he suggested. 'Is that what you're trying to say?'

She shrugged. 'Something like that.'

'And that's why you fell into my arms without so much as a murmur of opposition?'

Mia glanced over her shoulder but she couldn't read his expression. A little shiver ran down her spine all the same. 'Well…'

'Not because you really wanted it, because you couldn't help yourself or anything like that? Not because it was *us* and nothing else was going to work?'

There was no doubting the mockery in his voice now.

Mia trembled within. 'I'm sorry if I've offended you,' she said slowly and carefully.

'Because—' he sat up abruptly '—you needed some space to lick your wounds? Is *that* it, Mia?' he shot at her.

She stumbled to her feet. 'Yes. Probably. I haven't had time to analyse it but you don't have to make it sound so awful.'

He stood up behind her. 'How would you put it?' he asked harshly, putting his hands on her shoulders and spinning her round to face him.

She tripped over her feet and had to cling to him for a moment. 'As…as needing some warmth, some consolation,' she stammered. 'What's wrong with that?'

'It's a lie,' he said and gripped her shoulders again. 'That's what's wrong with it. You need me, we need each other now and nothing else is going to make sense.'

Mia could feel her temper rising. 'You can't dictate to me like this, Carlos. I'll make up my own mind.' And she pulled away.

He reached for her but she warded him off and ran down the beach towards the water's edge. 'Stay away from me, Carlos,' she warned.

He took absolutely no notice of her and she ran a bit further, quite unaware the tide was coming in until a rogue wavelet broke around her ankles and her feet sank into the sand. She put out her hands to steady herself but fell over, just in time to be doused by another wavelet.

'Mia, be careful!' Carlos lifted her up and set her on her feet. 'You're all wet and sandy. What did you think I was going to do to you?'

'*Kiss me,*' she said through her teeth. 'Kiss me and hold me and touch me until I don't know if I'm on my head or my heels and then persuade me to elope! But that's not fair, Carlos. I don't want to marry you.'

'Sure?' He asked it quite casually as he lifted her

and set her down further up the beach and out of the way of the incoming tide.

'No, of course I'm not sure,' she said irritably as she looked down at the sodden mess she was. 'There'd be lots of quite nice things about being married to you. None of them are the real reason for marriage, though.'

'Quite nice things such as Bellbird, such as playing ladies and imagining yourself on an Indian hill station? Such as kids when you want them and as many as you want?'

She clicked her tongue. 'Those were dreams. I never really expected them to come true.'

'All right, how about this, then? Such satisfactory sex you can't stop smiling?'

Mia bit her lip and inwardly cursed Carlos.

He went on. 'As for those real reasons you quote— I imagine being madly in love for ever and ever is numero uno?' He raised a dark eyebrow at her.

She nodded reluctantly.

'How are you supposed to know it's going to happen?' he enquired.

Mia stared up at him. 'It can happen. You sound as if you don't believe in it, but it happened for my parents.'

'It happened for my parents,' he said dryly. 'But *I* happen to think it's something that grows between two people. Do you see it happening for you? Has anyone got as far as this with you, Mia?'

'This?' she said uncertainly.

'Yes, this. I'm going to take you back to the motel now. I'm going to strip off your wet sandy clothes and put you in a warm shower. When you come out I'm

going to put you into bed with an extra blanket to keep
you warm and heap up the pillows. Then I'm going to
brew some of the excellent coffee they've provided.'

Mia simply stared up at him.

'When we've had that,' he went on, 'if we feel like
it, we can make slow, exquisite love to each other. Or
the wild and wanton variety we had last night. Or we
can just go to sleep together.

'Incidentally,' he added, 'I love the way you curl up
in my arms and go to sleep. I love the way you even
smile in your sleep.'

'I don't...I do?' she said huskily.

'You do. Look—' he shoved his hands into his pockets '—you could catch cold like this.'

She shivered right on cue.

Fortunately they hadn't driven to the beach. They'd just
collected the rug from the car, so Mia didn't have to
worry about the mess she would make in his car; the
motel and the thought of shedding damp sand all over
the place was another matter.

'Put your shoulders back, tilt your chin and just do
it, Mia,' he advised. 'It probably happens all the time.
Besides which, they're bound to have vacuum cleaners.'

She cast him a look that told him he might pay her
funny little compliments but he needn't think he was
forgiven for anything. In fact she was in just the right
mood to do as he suggested, put her shoulders back and
tilt her chin—at him, though.

'All right. Not so bad?' he said as he unlocked their
door and she stepped into the room. 'Next step,' he said

as she nodded reluctantly. 'Straight into the shower. You can rinse yourself and your clothes off,' he recommended with just a hint of amusement.

Mia went to say something along the lines of it all being his fault anyway but she resisted the temptation and marched into the bathroom and closed the door pointedly.

He opened it immediately.

She whirled round, her eyes sparkling a furious green.

'I just wanted to apologise and assure you I now have no intention of laying a finger on you,' he drawled. 'As for marrying you, it was only a thought, not a threat.' And he closed the door gently.

Mia rinsed her clothes thoroughly before showering and washing her hair. By the time she'd done all this the bathroom was well and truly steamed up and her skin was rosy. The only problem that remained was the fact that she had nothing to wear; she'd not taken that into account in her high dudgeon.

Her shoulders slumped as she stared at herself in the steamy mirror. What was she fighting about anyway? she wondered disconsolately. No one could force her to marry them. All she had to do was remove herself.

But… She sighed suddenly and closed her eyes. She was inextricably tied up with Bellbird for the next few months, something Carlos well knew.

What would it really be like to be married to Carlos

O'Connor? Of course there was only one way to find out, wasn't there? And was he right—love grew?

She wrapped a thick white towel around herself and opened the bathroom door.

Carlos was lying on top of the bed wearing only his boxers, resting his head on his elbow. There was a tray with a coffee plunger and cups on the bedside table next to him. There were pencil-thin little packets of sugar in a brown pottery bowl on the tray and some locally made cookies in cellophane wrappings.

He said nothing, just watched her advance towards the bed and his expression was entirely unreadable.

Mia reached the foot of the bed before she spoke. 'I don't know what you're thinking, Carlos, but I hate this kind of bickering. I mean, I don't like myself for... for going along with it so I'll just say this. I'm not sure of anything anymore. I can't make any decisions right now...and—' she pointed towards her pillows '—would you mind passing me my nightgown? By the way,' she sniffed, 'your coffee smells wonderful.'

His expression softened suddenly and he sat up and held out a hand to her.

She hesitated, then walked round the bed and took it. 'Hop in,' he invited.

'This towel is wet.'

'Ah.' He reached under her pillows and withdrew her nightgown, not her new one but an unexceptional sky-blue silky one with shoestring straps and kites all over it.

She loosened the towel and he told her to lift up her arms.

She did so obediently and he slipped the nightgown over her head and smoothed it down her body.

'There, all present and correct,' he murmured and studied the kites. 'Could even be fairly topical.'

'What do you mean?' She looked down.

'Assuming you lift the embargo you placed on me—' he ran his fingers through her damp hair '—we—'

'I placed no embargo on you,' she broke in.

'You told me, through gritted teeth,' he contradicted, 'that I had a habit of kissing you and holding you and touching you until you didn't know if you were on your head or your heels.'

Mia drew an exasperated breath. 'All the same...I mean, that's not an embargo.'

'No,' he agreed. 'Still, no decent guy would fail to realise you disapproved of not knowing if you were on your head or your heels, and therefore desist.'

Mia stared at him almost cross-eyed as she tried to work out what he was getting at. 'What has this got to do with my nightgown?' she asked finally in a heavily frustrated voice.

'Kites,' he replied succinctly.

She blinked.

'I see you still don't understand.' He put his finger on her chin and smiled at her. 'We could reach for the sky like your kites—if we were friends and lovers. That's why it seemed topical.'

Mia stayed perfectly still for about half a minute. That was as long as she could maintain her sobriety and prevent a smile from curving her lips.

'You're quite mad, you know,' she told him.

'Maybe,' he agreed perfectly seriously, 'but am I forgiven?'

'Yes.'

'Come in then.'

She climbed into bed and said in a heartfelt way, 'That's much better.'

'Better?'

'Than fighting. Don't you think?'

'Yes.' He put his arms around her but she didn't see the faint frown in his eyes as he looked over her head.

A couple of hours later, Mia was fast asleep but once again Carlos found himself watching her as she slept.

They had made love, not the wild, wanton variety but it had been warm and sensuous all the same. She was generous and delicious as a lover and she came down from the heights in a way that aroused his protective instincts.

In fact, it occurred to him that he wouldn't like to think of her vulnerability at those times in another man's hands. Someone who didn't realise she gave it her all, like she did so much in her life.

He'd got up when he'd found he couldn't sleep and gone outside into the garden. He'd heard the surf pounding on the beach and the breeze sighing through the Norfolk pines that lined the road. He'd listened to it for a time before he'd come back inside and pulled on a sweatshirt and pushed an armchair over towards the bed.

And, as he watched, he thought back to her as a girl. A girl who'd loved nothing better than to ride like the wind whenever she came home. Almost as if, he mused, her horse and the breeze through that tangled mop of dark hair released her from the constraints of her boarding school.

She'd been a shy child—you wouldn't have known she was there until you caught glimpses of her on the estate.

Then, when she was about fifteen, he reckoned, they'd started riding together when he was home. It had happened quite coincidentally and not often but after a while he'd noticed on the odd occasion that she coloured slightly when he spoke to her.

He'd done nothing other than limiting his visits to West Windward if he knew she'd be home, said nothing and hoped it would go away for her.

Only to get hit on the head by a falling branch in a wild storm and to discover Mia Gardiner was no longer a kid. Not only that, but she was a luscious eighteen-year-old and eminently desirable.

She was still luscious and desirable but there was a lot more to it now. She was clever, she was spirited, she'd fashioned a successful career for herself that didn't depend on her looks—if his father had been alive to see Mia Gardiner now, he would approve of her much more than he'd ever approved of Nina French.

He grimaced as this thought came to him. Contrary to his wife's opinion on the matter, Frank O'Connor had deemed Nina French to be a lovely clothes horse with an empty head and without the internal fortitude to make a good wife and mother.

Not that his father's sentiments had surprised him. But they had, unfortunately, he reflected, sent him down a path he was now very much regretting. In fact he was not only regretful but guilty, he thought sombrely.

Of course the irony of it all hadn't failed to strike him either. Nina had very much wanted to marry him. Mia did not.

He stared across the bed at a dim rim of light below the bathroom door. Why had he brought marriage into the equation like throwing a hat in the ring?

What kind of a marriage did he envisage with Mia, anyway?

A peaceful one. A marriage to a woman who was practical, clever, resourceful and artistic. Someone who loved kids—his mother should appreciate that, always assuming he could ever get his mother to appreciate anything about Mia.

A marriage with her living at Bellbird and him coming and going as he saw fit. None of the highs and lows of his relationship with Nina—none of the insidious feelings that marriage to Nina would be like a never-ending grand opera. And of course Mia being forever grateful for the way he'd redeemed himself, and his family.

He set his teeth because it was an unpleasant thought.

But there had to be something more to it all, he

reflected. The answer that came was not much help to him.

There was something about Mia Gardiner that got under his skin.

CHAPTER SEVEN

MIA WOKE THE next morning with no idea what to expect.

But, unaware that Carlos had been up half the night wrestling with his demons, she was surprised to find him fast asleep despite the sunlight filtering into the room, courtesy of the curtains they'd forgotten to close.

She watched him for a while and wondered why she should not exactly be uneasy about what today would bring but have a question mark in her mind.

Last night had ended well, she thought, and felt a rush of colour in her cheeks. *Ended well* was a strange phrase to use to describe an encounter that had left her on cloud nine and aware of her body in ever new and divinely sensual ways.

What if Carlos wanted to talk about marriage again? How would she respond in the cold light of day?

She shook her head and decided to go for a swim, thinking that maybe it would wash away all her uncertainties.

She slipped out of bed and padded to the bathroom, where she put on her black-and-white bikini and her white terry robe. When she came back into the room he was still fast asleep.

She blew him a kiss.

It was a fabulous morning. A high blue sky had followed the burnt orange of dawn as the sun rose and the surface of the water was glassy. It was about half tide and long gentle breakers were rolling in to the beach, perfect for body-surfing.

Mia dropped her robe, ran into the water and dived cleanly beneath the first breaker she came to.

Half an hour later, she emerged to find Carlos sitting on the beach wearing board shorts but looking moody.

'Hi.' She picked up her towel. 'The water is amazing. Don't you want to go in?'

'I do and I don't. Would you mind not dripping all over me?'

Mia clicked her tongue and hid a smile. 'Sorry.' She spread out her towel and sat down on it. 'I'll come with you if you like.'

'You think I might need my hand held?' he asked with some animosity. 'I've been surfing since I was six.'

She put her hand over his. 'Not that kind of a hand. The hand of friendship, I meant. Some days when you wake up feeling sour and cranky, it helps.'

She lifted his hand and kissed his palm, then folded his fingers over it and gave him his hand back. 'There!'

And she got up and ran down the beach and back into the water.

He wasn't far behind her.

* * *

'You're a genius,' Carlos said later, over breakfast. 'I got up fully prepared—' he paused and buttered his toast '—to be mean and miserable today. Now look what you've done.' He smoothed some marmalade onto the toast.

They were eating at a beachside café renowned for their breakfast. They both wore jeans and T-shirts. Mia had tied her hair back with a floral scarf.

'I'm glad,' she said, and smiled.

'Still on the smiley trail,' he commented.

'Still on the smiley trail,' she agreed but sobered. 'What are you doing today?'

'Why?'

'I thought I'd go up to Lismore and see my parents, but you don't need to come.'

'I would come but in fact I've got some guys to see this morning—you'd be amazed who ends up in Byron,' he said a shade ruefully. 'But they're actually involved with the equestrian centre, so it's a good opportunity. Take the car.'

'Oh, I thought I'd hire a car.' She poured some coffee and sniffed appreciatively. 'More delicious coffee.'

'This is grown in the area, around Newrybar, I believe. Take the car,' he repeated.

'I've never driven a sports car.'

'So long as you can drive a manual you'll be fine.' She hesitated.

'Mia, do you have any idea what an honour this is?'

'Honour?' She looked around bewilderedly, at the

wooden table and benches, at the other breakfasters and the beach over the railing.

'Not this place,' he told her. 'But I have never offered my car to a woman to drive.'

She stared at him with parted lips. Then she had to laugh. 'If you think that makes me feel any better about it, you're mistaken.' She paused. 'But thanks, anyway.'

'Don't forget we've got a date tonight,' were his last words to her before she set off for Lismore.

'I won't! Thanks again,' she called back and with a surge of exhilaration swung his beautiful little car into the street.

Mia arrived back late afternoon, safe and sound from her trip to Lismore and without putting so much as the tiniest scratch on his car.

She was happy with the state of mind she'd found her parents in and the news that her father would be leaving hospital shortly.

She was greeted on her return with the news that Carlos had gone to Queensland.

'Gone to Queensland?' she repeated to the receptionist who had waylaid her. 'Are you serious?'

'Just over the border by helicopter to look at an equestrian centre. Apparently he's developing one down south and he wanted to see if he could get any ideas from this one. He asked me to explain that to you, Miss Gardiner, and to assure you he'll be back in time for your dinner date this evening.'

'Oh. Well, thanks.'

* * *

That had been a few hours ago and Mia was now almost dressed for dinner, although there was still no sign of Carlos.

She was sitting at the dressing table contemplating her hair.

Whereas this time yesterday she'd had a most elegant and intricate style wrought by a hairdresser, she'd washed her hair twice lately, once last night after getting rolled over in the wet sand and once this morning after her swim. Therefore her hair was no longer sleek; it was wild and curly. With an inward sigh she decided there was only one solution—to tie it back severely.

But she stayed where she was when she'd finished, staring at her image unseeingly as she fiddled with her brush and recalled her parents' unspoken curiosity on the subject of her and Carlos.

Assuming she had to explain things to them, she thought, what would she say? *He actually asked me to marry him but I said no.* Why? *Because I still sense... I don't know...I can't forget what he said or how he looked when he talked about Nina in the restaurant at Blackheath that night.*

Why? Because it struck me—and he didn't so much ask me as suggest we get married—that it was a testing the waters sort of proposal. A thought, not a threat, maybe another unreal aspect of our relationship.

And, for all the happiness he's brought me, there's still a shadow of something in him, be it Nina or...

Her eyes widened suddenly as Carlos strolled in and stood behind her so she was looking at his reflection.

'Hi,' he said. 'Penny for them?'

'What do you mean?' she asked huskily.

'I was watching you from the doorway before you caught sight of me. You were deep in serious thought.'

Mia stood up and smoothed her dress down. 'I was beginning to think you'd forgotten about me.'

'No.' He caught her in his arms. 'I've been thinking about you all day, it so happens. And half the night,' he added a shade dryly.

She cupped his cheek. 'Is that why you woke up in a bad mood?' she asked wryly.

'It was myself I was cranky with. Hey—' he looked down at her '—what have you done to your hair?'

She explained.

'But I like it wild and curly.' He raised his hands and started to take out the clips.

'Carlos!' She stopped.

'Mia?' He raised an eyebrow at her and continued to take out the clips.

She grimaced. 'I guess it's a waste of time asking you to desist?'

'Yes. There.' He presented her with a little bundle of clips and ran his fingers through her loosened hair.

'Is there anything else you don't approve of?' she queried.

'About you?'

'Yes, me. I just thought I ought to be prepared in case you decide to wreak further havoc with my appearance.'

'No,' he said simply as he looked her up and down. 'Well, much as I am looking forward to removing your lovely blue dress and allowing myself the pleasure of parting your thighs, running my fingers over your breasts and round your hips, I'll wait.'

Mia all but choked. 'I'm glad to hear it,' she said with difficulty.

He raised an eyebrow again at her. 'You don't approve?'

'Oh—' she tossed her head '—I approve. That's the problem. But if you can wait, so can I.'

And she turned on her heel and walked away from him.

He caught her and turned her in his arms. 'On second thoughts,' he growled, 'I don't think I can. We've still got time.'

She took a ragged breath.

'We've—' he looked at his watch '—got nearly an hour. Half an hour until the table is booked, half an hour or a bit less to be fashionably late.'

'Carlos,' she breathed but she couldn't go on—for several reasons. She had no idea what she'd been going to say and it was impossible to think straight as he ran his hands from the rounded curves of her shoulders down her arms.

He still wore the jeans and shirt he'd put on after their swim, clothes he'd been wearing all day, and she was assaulted by the pure man smell she'd always loved about Carlos, musk and cotton and something that was so masculine she just loved it.

Then he found the zip of her dress and the material parted down her back and the dress pooled on the floor at her feet.

He made a husky sound of approval in his throat as

she stood before him wearing only her blue silk and lace panties and her beautiful high blue sandals. And his grey gaze lingered on her slim waist, on her thighs and on the smooth hollows at the base of her throat where a telltale nerve was beating a tattoo.

Then he moved forward and cupped her breasts and bent his head to tease her nipples with his tongue and teeth.

Mia went rigid as wave after wave of sensation and desire crashed through her body, and he picked her up and laid her on the bed.

This time there was no time for any more formalities, this time they were both ignited to a fever pitch and desperate for each other. This time it took Carlos as long to come down from the heights as it did Mia.

'That,' he said eventually and still breathing heavily, 'is a record. In as much as we could still shower, get dressed again and be on time for our reservation.'

Mia chuckled. 'We could also sit down and die at the table. I think I'd rather be late.'

He rearranged the pillows, then pulled her back into his arms. 'OK?'

She nodded.

He kissed the tip of her nose. Then he looked into her eyes wryly. 'Realistically, I suspect we're not going to make dinner.' He looked a question at her.

'You suspect right,' she told him. 'I don't feel like getting all done up again.' She snuggled up to him. 'I just feel like staying here.'

He smoothed some strands of hair from her cheek. 'Why not?'

So that was what they did—stayed in bed, with Carlos watching television with the sound turned down and Mia dozing next to him.

Then, at about eleven o'clock, they decided they were starving so they got up and dressed in jeans and sweaters and ran down the motel stairs to the ground floor, hand in hand, and out into the moonlight.

They found a small packed restaurant vibrating with blues music and serving late dinners.

Mia had pasta, Carlos had ocean-fresh prawns and they drank Chianti. Every now and then they got up and joined the crowd on the minuscule dance floor until last orders were called, then they walked to the beach.

'Still OK?' He swung her hand. 'Still on the smiley trail?'

She stopped walking and looked up at him. 'Yes.'

He responded to her rather intent look with a quizzical one of his own. 'You were going to say?' he hazarded.

Mia licked her lips. *I was going to say yes, I will marry you, Carlos. I couldn't not marry you. It would be like sentencing myself to purgatory. I almost got it out but I can't quite bring myself to say it. Why can't I?*

She said, 'What will we do tomorrow?' and inwardly called herself a coward.

He studied her expressionlessly for a long moment, then he shrugged and they started walking again. 'If you think Gail can spare you for another day we could drive up to the Goldie and have a look around.'

'You mean the Gold Coast?'

'Uh-huh.'

'All right. As for Gail—' she dimpled '—she is in seventh heaven—and she's doing marvellously well. She's got her mother helping and Bill's wife, Lucy. I'm proud of her.'

'You probably trained her well,' he commented. 'Ready for bed? Again?' he asked whimsically.

'Considering it's three o'clock in the morning, yes!'

But they didn't go anywhere the next day. Instead they swam and lazed around and enjoyed each other's company.

That evening they were seated at a table for two in the luxurious restaurant next door to their motel. Mia was wearing her new blue dress.

'Third time lucky,' she'd said to Carlos earlier, when she was dressed and ready to go.

He smiled down at her. 'You look marvellous. So does your hair.'

She'd left her hair loose and riotous. 'You know,' she said to him, 'you could make my life much simpler.' She paused and looked suddenly rueful.

'I have been trying to make that point,' he replied as he shrugged into the jacket of his navy suit, worn with a crisp white shirt and a navy tie. His dark hair was thick but orderly and secretly he took her breath away.

'I meant my hair. I wouldn't have to worry so much about it.'

He closed in on her and tilted her chin with his fingers. 'That should be the least of your worries,' he said softly, but scanned her significantly from head to toe.

'Now you've really got me seriously concerned,' she said with an anxious expression. 'Did I speak too soon?'

'About getting to dinner in your new blue dress?' He let his words hang in the air, then took her hand with a wicked little smile in his eyes. 'Get me out of here, Miss Gardiner, just to be on the safe side.'

They dined on lobster and they drank champagne.

Mia was just making up her mind whether to have dessert when she looked up from the menu to see Carlos staring past her, looking pale and with his expression as hard as a rock.

She didn't have to turn to see what had engaged his attention so dramatically. Nina French swept up to their table and there was no mistaking her or, after a startled moment, the man she was with—Talbot Spencer.

Nina was eminently photogenic but in the flesh she was breathtakingly beautiful, with the finest skin, velvety blue eyes and long smooth-flowing corn-gold hair. She was wearing a floral sheath dress that clung to her figure and was held up by shoestring straps so that it just covered her breasts. High nude platform shoes complemented her legs. Above all she had a tiny smile curving her lips, not of triumph or mockery, but a genuine smile.

Talbot wore a suit and Mia had to admit that, fair and freckled, he was also dangerously attractive, although in a way she couldn't quite put her finger on.

It was Nina who broke the startled silence. 'Hi there, Carlos. This is a surprise. I guess you know Talbot, but please introduce me to your friend.'

Carlos stood up and probably only Mia noticed that

his knuckles were white as he put his napkin on the table. 'Nina, Talbot,' he drawled. 'You're right, this is a surprise. Didn't know you two knew each other. Uh... this is Mia Gardiner. Mia,' he went on, 'and I are contemplating getting married, so wish us luck.'

The silence that crashed down around them was deafening.

Nina's expression spoke volumes although she said not a word. She looked horrified; her face actually crumpled and her beautiful blue eyes filled with tears.

It was Talbot who broke the silence. 'That's an interesting way of putting it. Do let us know the outcome of your contemplations. We're off back to Sydney tomorrow—maybe we could get together down there? Nice to meet you, Mia! Come, Nina.'

Nina swallowed, then turned obediently and followed him out of the restaurant.

Carlos sat down but immediately stood up. 'Let's get out of here,' he said tersely.

'Th-the bill,' Mia stammered.

'Don't worry about it, they know me. Ready?'

It wasn't to the beach he took her. They drove up to the lighthouse instead. In silence.

It was cool and dark, the moon hidden by a thick blanket of clouds.

'It's going to rain tomorrow, the end of our idyll, Mia. In more ways than one, I suspect.' He turned to her and slid his arm along the back of her seat. 'Go ahead, say it. I can guess anyway—how *could* you, Carlos?'

Mia cleared her throat. 'Yes,' she agreed huskily, 'I was, and I'm still going to say it. How could you?'

He raised a sardonic eyebrow at her. 'It isn't true? I've certainly been contemplating marrying you, Mia. I could have sworn you might even have been having second thoughts about it.'

Mia bit her lip and tried desperately to gather some remnants of sane rational composure around her. 'Carlos,' she said as she battled more tears, 'do you think linking up with Talbot Spencer was a calculated move on Nina's part to get back at you for breaking up with her?'

'Yes, I do,' he said dryly.

'Have you spoken to her since you broke up?'

'No.'

'Has she tried to speak to you?'

'Mia, she was the one who broke it off,' he said tersely. Then he shrugged. 'She's left messages,' he said sombrely, and added, 'I've been overseas most of the time.' He took a breath and said through his teeth. 'Anyone but Talbot!'

'I don't think so.' Mia closed her eyes and tried to concentrate. 'I think whoever it was, you'd hate the idea of it because—' she gestured helplessly '—there's still something between you two. From the way she looked, there certainly is for *her*. But whatever, none of this is about *me*, don't you see? I've been like a sideshow to the main attraction through all this and it's not something I care to be any more.'

Despite her tear streaks he could see the determination in her eyes and the set of her mouth, and he cursed inwardly.

'Mia…' he paused, and his tone was harsh as he continued '…there's something you don't understand. I will probably always feel guilty about Nina unless I can see her genuinely happy with another man.'

'Guilty?' Mia whispered. 'Why?'

'Because she quite inadvertently became a hostage in my war with my father.'

'You're right. I…I don't understand,' Mia stammered.

Carlos rubbed his face. 'He didn't approve of her.'

Mia did a double take. 'He must have been the only one!'

He grimaced. 'Possibly. But because I thought he was running true to form, finding fault with my choices simply on principle, I wanted to prove him wrong.

'But he was right. Well—' he shrugged '—I don't know if she'll ever make a good wife and mother, but underneath the initial attraction, and you'd have to be a block of wood not to be attracted to her,' he said with obvious bitterness, 'we were never really compatible, Nina and I, only I refused to admit it because I couldn't bear to think my father was right and I was wrong.'

Mia stared at him incredulously.

'And in the process,' he continued bleakly, 'I guess I gave Nina a false sense of security—if not that, I obviously led her to believe that whatever she did, I'd always be there for her. In a way she was entitled to think I'd marry her. And for that I will always feel guilty. And now she's fallen into Talbot's clutches.'

He raked a hand through his hair, then, as she shivered, he took his jacket off and put it round her shoulders.

Mia hugged herself beneath his jacket and came to a decision. 'I...I can't help thinking—I'm sorry but I still believe you haven't got over her and maybe you never will.'

'Mia—'

'No,' she interrupted. 'Please, you must listen to me. I can't be a party to breaking Nina French's heart, or taking you to a place you don't really want to go, not in *your* heart.'

There was a long silence as they looked painfully into each other's eyes. Then he said, 'It's been good, though?'

Mia thought back over the last few days and nodded. 'Yes, yes, it's been lovely.' She wiped her eyes on her wrists.

'Don't cry.' He slipped his jacket off her and pulled her into his arms. 'Don't cry, please.' He kissed the top of her head. 'I feel bad enough as it is.'

'You don't need to.'

'I can't leave you like this.'

'Carlos, you can—for once in my life I didn't bring a tissue or a hanky!' she exclaimed frustratedly.

'Here.' He pulled a clean navy hanky out of his trouser pocket.

She mopped up and blew her nose. 'What was I saying? Yes, you can.' Mia paused and dredged the very depths of her soul for the right words, the right key to handle this, to bring it to a closure that would release not only her, but Carlos without him realising how much she loved him.

'Have you ever seen the Three Sisters?'

Carlos blinked. 'At Echo Point?'

'Mmm-hmm…' She nodded.

'Well, yes.' But he looked mystified.

'I used to feel a bit like them.' Mia dabbed at her eyes again. 'Sort of frozen and petrified. As if I could never break the bonds of what happened at West Windward.'

She hesitated, still searching for the right words. She stared out to sea, but all she could see was a dark blue world.

'Now, thanks to you, I feel different,' she said slowly. 'I feel I can go ahead. It's funny because she'd absolutely hate the thought of it, but what you've done for me is remove the stamp your mother put on me that kept me trapped like that.'

He was silent. But the lines and angles of his face spoke volumes too; he looked harsh and forbidding but at the same time tortured.

'But—' Mia took a deep breath '—this is a real parting of the ways for us. You do see, don't you?' she pleaded.

'You don't believe you're sending me back to Nina, do you?' he asked roughly.

Mia put a finger to his lips. 'That's not for me to do,' she said huskily. 'Only you can work that out. But I think you *have* to work it out. I just want you to know you don't have to worry about me.'

He took her hand and kissed her palm and, as she had done only the day before, closed her fingers over her palm.

'I can only do this one way, Mia.'

She looked a question at him with silent tears slipping down her cheeks.

'Now, tonight. I'll take you back to the motel, then drive on to Sydney. I can organise transport back for you whenever you want it.'

She licked the tears off her lips. 'That's fine. Thanks.'

'Mia—'

'No, you mustn't worry about me.'

'You're crying again,' he said harshly.

'Most women probably have a man they remember with a tear and a smile. The one that got away,' she said whimsically. 'But, believe me, it's the way I want it.'

He stared into her eyes and found them unwavering. He closed his eyes briefly.

She leant over and brushed his lips with hers. 'Still—' she managed a brief but radiant smile '—we don't need to prolong things.'

They didn't.

Carlos drove them back to the motel, consulted over the bill, and it only took him ten minutes to pack. He changed into jeans and a tweed jacket.

Then it was all done and Mia stood straight and tearless in her lovely blue dress before him. 'Bye, now,' she said barely audibly. 'Please just go, but—*vaya con dios.*'

His face softened at the Spanish salutation and he hesitated, closed his eyes briefly and said, 'You too, Mia. You too.' Then he was gone.

Mia stayed where she was for a few minutes, too

scared to move in case she fractured and broke like glass. But of course it didn't happen.

You just go on, she thought as she lay down on the bed and pulled a pillow into her arms. You just go on and hope the pain goes away. You just know you couldn't go through the hoping and the dreaming—and the slamming back to earth again.

The Pacific Highway between Byron Bay and Sydney was at times narrow and tortuous, almost always busy. Not an easy drive at the best of times. Late at night in wet conditions behind the monotonous click of the windscreen wipers with spray coming up off the road from oncoming traffic, it required skill and concentration.

It didn't stop Carlos from thinking that he'd displayed little skill in his dealings with Mia. After the encounter with Nina and Talbot, who could blame her for withdrawing from the lists?

After revealing that Nina had known what she was doing in linking up with his enemy and after their tit-for-tat exchange and the way Nina had looked was enough to make anyone believe there was unfinished business between them.

Was there? he wondered suddenly. Other than the explanation he undoubtedly owed Nina? Could he ever go back to that emotional roller coaster he'd shared with Nina French?

It struck him suddenly that he might have if he hadn't run into Mia again. He might have allowed the familiarity of their routine to draw him back to her; the guilt he felt towards her might have made him do it.

The irony was that now he knew he couldn't go back to her, the reason for it—Mia, who smiled in her sleep—was apparently prepared to sleep with him but not to marry him.

Could he blame her? No. Her shock on hearing how he'd used Nina in the war with his father—had that recalled memories of the way she'd been treated back at West Windward?

Had those fears ever left her—that it could happen to her again in some way? Would they ever leave her? Yes, she'd slept with him, but had she ever really opened her heart to him?

She certainly hadn't shown any great excitement at the thought of racing to the altar with him.

But here he was, racing back to Sydney to stop Nina French from getting entangled with Talbot Spencer—why?

Because he had a guilt complex? No doubt about it.

Because he needed to exorcise himself of the demons that his father as well as Nina had left him with so he could go back to Mia without any baggage.

But how to do that? If she really meant it was over?

CHAPTER EIGHT

FOUR MONTHS LATER Mia sat at her desk on her last day at Bellbird.

She'd held her last function the day before and a van now stood outside the house, ready to remove all the equipment she'd hired on a year to year basis, tables, chairs, trolleys and linen. Another truck had removed the commercial kitchen equipment and all the crockery and cutlery.

Her office was unusually tidy. All her paperwork was filed and boxed, all her notes on the wall had gone.

All that was left, in fact, was her phone, a pen and a pad.

It had been a successful four months in that she'd managed to fulfil all her obligations. She had quite an extensive file of references for her next venture but, as it turned out, the glowing terms for her entertaining skills in those references were not going to be much help to her at all as things stood at the moment.

She'd neither seen nor heard from Carlos. All her dealings had been with his secretary, Carol Manning, and no more functions had been booked for O'Connor Construction.

She'd held her breath and felt like fainting for a moment when she'd been idly scanning a newspaper and seen an article entitled: O'Connor Wedding Goes Without Hitch Despite Weather.

Carlos and Nina, a voice of doom had said in her head. But when she'd opened her eyes and forced herself to read, it wasn't Carlos O'Connor who'd got married—it was his mother!

She'd read on, astounded. 'Arancha O'Connor, widow of construction billionaire Frank O'Connor, had remarried in an elegant ceremony despite highly inclement weather, with her son Carlos and her daughter Juanita by her side. Her new husband,' the article continued, 'was a chef, and he had made the wedding cake.'

Mia had choked on nothing to the extent that Gail heard her coughing and came and banged her on the back, then brought her a glass of water.

'What?'

'I don't believe it!'

'Don't believe what?' Gail asked.

'His mother has married a chef!'

'Always handy to have a chef in the house,' Gail had commented. 'Whose mother?'

Mia took a mouthful of water. 'Carlos.'

'Oh, him.' Gail had shrugged. Carlos had never regained his stellar status in her estimation. 'I remember her. Small, dark, big hat. Almost regal.' She'd looked at Mia curiously. 'Is there anything wrong with marrying a chef, though?'

'Yes. No, of course not, not in the normal course of events, but—' Mia had stopped, breathing heavily.

'That explains that. Yes and no. Clear as mud.'

Mia had to laugh. 'She…she could be quite snooty.'

Now, a few weeks after Arancha's wedding and the day before Mia left, not even Gail was with her.

She'd moved down to Sydney and taken up a position in a top hotel restaurant.

Bill and Lucy were staying on as caretakers and keepers of the garden; Bill was looking forward to having his autonomy handed back to him.

Not even Long John was with her; she'd given him to Harry Castle, the only person apart from her and Gail the horse didn't bite.

Now don't get maudlin, she warned herself as the last of the trucks drove off and she had the place more or less to herself. *What I'll do is—play ladies.*

She stood up and looked down at herself. She was wearing a long, full floral skirt with a white broderie anglaise blouse. Her hair was tied back in one thick, heavy bunch at the back. She even had a wide-brimmed lacy straw hat which a guest she hadn't been able to trace had left behind.

She also had a Royal Albert tea service, patterned with roses, one of Bellbird's heirlooms; she did have tea and a lemon on the tree beside the back door and she did have a kettle.

Ten minutes later, she'd pulled a wicker chair onto the front veranda, she had a small round wicker table beside her and a cup of lemon tea on it as she watched the late afternoon sun cast its lengthening shadows over the summer gardens of Bellbird and Mount Wilson. Her hat lay on a second chair.

She sipped her tea then put her cup down. Breathe this in, she told herself. *May some dim deep memory of the lovely peace of Bellbird always be with me.* She closed her eyes. *May the association it will always hold with Carlos bear no bitter memories for me.*

A car drove up.

She had to be dreaming, but didn't she know the sound of that engine off by heart? Didn't he *always* manage to kick up the gravel when he stopped?

She opened her eyes and it was Carlos.

Her hands flew to her mouth. 'It is you!' she whispered. 'I thought I must be dreaming.'

He propped a foot against the bottom step and leant against the rail. He wore cargo pants and a navy shirt. His dark hair was wind-blown; he must have had the car roof down at some stage. And, just at the sight of him, her heart started to beat heavily and her pulse raced. And for a moment she could smell the sea air, hear the surf and see in her mind's eye the wrinkled ocean below the lighthouse on Cape Byron....

He said, 'I couldn't let you go without making sure you were OK.'

He stopped and took in the lovely china on the wicker table beside her, the hat, and he half-smiled. 'Playing ladies?'

She grimaced. 'Being silly really, but yes.'

'Where are you going, Mia?'

'I...' She took a breath. 'To my parents for a while.'

'I thought they were driving around Australia.'

'They are. So their house is empty. I can stay as long as I like. But it'll only be until…' she plaited her fingers '…I get organised again.'

He watched her twining fingers as a faint frown grew in his eyes.

'So nothing definite in the pipeline at the moment?'

'Uh…one or two. These things take time to set up, though, Carlos.' She tried to look casual and unfazed as she said it but the truth of the matter was she had absolutely nothing in the pipeline.

Hard as she'd tried to get motivated and to move her life and her career forward, she hadn't succeeded—not something she was prepared to admit, however.

'By the way, I read about your mother!' she said in a bid to change the subject completely.

'She surprised the life out of us but they seem to be blissfully happy, even if he is only a chef, although—' he looked amused '—she insists he's a "celebrity" chef.' He rubbed his jaw ruefully. 'And she's like a different person. Much more contented.'

'I was going to say good,' Mia murmured with a tiny smile, 'but on second thoughts I won't say a word. Uh—how's Juanita?'

'She's fine. She's pregnant. Another cause for contentment in our mutual parent.'

Mia smiled. 'That's great news.'

'How are you getting to your parents' place?'

'I bought myself a four-wheel-drive station-wagon. I can fit all my stuff into it. I haven't got that much.'

He raised an eyebrow. 'Not Long John, though. Will you send him by horse transport?' He grinned suddenly. 'That should be jolly. Does he bite other horses as well as people?'

She dimpled and told him about Harry Castle.

'That's better,' he said.

Mia looked enquiringly at him. 'What?'

'I haven't seen those dimples for a while.'

'They…must come and go. Oh, by the way, I've left an inventory of all the china and stuff. You probably should go through it with me now.'

'No. It doesn't matter.'

'But there's some beautiful stuff.'

'Help yourself if you want any of it. And so can Bill and Lucy, for that matter, Gail's mother too.'

'That's nice but don't you…you don't care about it, do you?' she hazarded with a look of something like pain in her eyes at the thought of Bellbird being summarily stripped of its treasures, even if they were going to people she knew. Not that they were worth a fortune or anything like that, but they were old and they were lovely.

Carlos straightened and folded his arms. 'Mia, you didn't want Bellbird. You couldn't have made that plainer. So it's going on the market again. As soon as you leave.'

It was like an arrow going through her heart. She gasped and went white.

He swore under his breath. 'What did you think I'd do with it? What do you think I ought to do with it?' he asked harshly.

'You told me it was nice enough for that to be sufficient reason to buy it.'

'Not if you're not going to live on it.'

'Carlos, I thought it would be safe with you,' she said passionately. 'Safe from people who'd tear the house down and put up something modern. Safe from developers and sub-division. You never know when that can happen.'

'It's not going to happen up here in the foreseeable future, Mia.'

She subsided but started plaiting her fingers again.

'You're not having second thoughts, are you?'

She swallowed and turned her head away.

'Mia, look at me,' he commanded softly. 'Are you?'

'No.' She said it barely audibly but quite definitely.

'Then what are you so upset about? Just leaving here?'

'I…I was doing fine until you turned up. Indulging in a little gentle melancholy, perhaps—' she grimaced '—but mostly under control. Tell me about *you*.'

He came up the steps, lifted her hat off the chair and sat down, putting the hat on the floor beside him. 'Nina married Talbot.'

Mia moved convulsively. 'Why?' she whispered. 'Why did you let her? Why was there no publicity?'

'You'd have to ask her why,' he said dryly. 'As for letting her, how could I stop her? And, lastly, they tied the knot overseas; in fact, they've moved overseas.'

Mia stared at him. 'But she looked so devastated. That night at Byron.'

'Nina's good at that.'

'But she looked so…I can't put my finger on why,

but she looked so nice, I mean, as if she's a thoroughly nice person!'

'She is, most of the time. But buried under that is a too-beautiful-for-her-own-good girl who's been spoilt rotten.' He shrugged. 'You never know, Talbot may just be the one to cope with her. She may even be the one to bring out the best in him. Strangely, I saw them at the airport recently. They looked—' he gestured '—happy.'

'Are you sick at heart?' Mia asked. 'Surely you can tell me.'

He picked up her hat and twirled it around. 'To be honest, I'm relieved. I know I wasn't at first, but Talbot always brought out the worst in me.' He thought for a moment. 'I don't know if she was on the rebound, I probably will never know, but one thing I do know, *I* couldn't have made it work for us. If I hadn't known that intrinsically I wouldn't have held out against marrying her for so long.'

Not quite the same as saying he didn't love her, nor did it mean he didn't still love her, Mia thought, and wondered what would be worse—to know Nina was unhappy with Talbot, or happy?'

She got up and walked to the edge of the veranda. The hydrangeas that rimmed the veranda and had looked so good in the Wedgwood soup tureen were dying off now. In general, the gardens were on their last summer legs, as Bill put it.

She looked out and shaded her eyes against the sun and she could suddenly visualise the gardens being allowed to run wild, the property being sub-divided, the house being altered or simply neglected and she thought she couldn't bear it…

'Would you…w-would you…' her voice shook '…would you consider going into a business partnership with me, Carlos?'

She heard the startled hiss of his breath and steeled herself for rejection, scorn, anger or all three.

'What do you mean?' he said harshly.

She turned round slowly and swallowed twice as she tried to marshal her thoughts. 'I made a small success of the business I ran here, I guess you could say, but it was always a bit of a battle. I only managed to start it with a bank loan and I was always having to plough most of the profits into loan repayments and lease payments. But with a partner, especially one who owned the place, I could really—' she twisted her hands '—go onto bigger and better things.'

'Like what?'

'Like upgrading the furniture and fittings. They're starting to get shabby. Like live music, such as a classical quartet for functions, or live jazz or live modern, but really good stuff. Like children's birthday parties.' She paused.

He frowned.

'I mean special parties with a marquee, a carousel, castles, fairies or, for boys, cowboy themes and pony rides. We could set it up in the west paddock. I have a theory that real class attracts real money and I think I could make the Bellbird Estate more than pay its way for you by going really upmarket, but with imagination and…well…' she looked a bit embarrassed '…flair.'

All she could hear in the silence that followed were the bellbirds calling.

'Another thought I had was a honeymoon suite. There's a marvellous view from the east paddock. You could build a luxury cottage for the bride and groom to spend their first night in, with open fireplaces and gourmet meals. Is—' her eyes were wary '—there any point in me going on?'

'All right,' he said at last. 'If that's how you want it, so be it. I'll get the paperwork drawn up.' He stood up and handed her the hat. 'You can unpack, Miss Gardiner.'

Mia stared up at him with her heart in her mouth because something was radically different about him. It was as if a shutter had come down and she couldn't read him anymore except to see how cold his eyes were now.

'Carlos,' she said involuntarily, then stopped and bit her lip.

'Mia?' He raised an eyebrow. 'You were saying?'

'I…no, nothing,' she stammered.

'Nothing,' he repeated. He lifted a hand and touched his knuckles to the point of her chin. 'Nothing's changed, I guess. I'll be in touch. Or Carol will.' And he moved past her, jogged down the steps and, minutes later, his car roared away.

'What have I done?' Mia asked aloud. 'Oh, what have I done?'

CHAPTER NINE

SIX MONTHS LATER Mia and Gail were engaged in a conference about an upcoming function—a christening.

Mia had not so much pinched Gail from her upmarket job, she'd welcomed her back with open arms. Gail had been miserable down in Sydney.

The first thing Mia had done, after gathering herself together following her encounter with Carlos on the day before she'd been supposed to leave, had been to advertise and send out flyers to previous customers to the effect that the Bellbird Estate was reopening shortly after some renovations and with some new attractions.

For the next couple of months her life had been spent on the redecorating trail and consulting with architects, designers and builders.

The house had been finished first and it was gratifying to find she was almost booked up for the first month.

Then the honeymoon suite had been completed and their first couple to spend the first night of their marriage in it were so impressed they'd wanted to stay on.

The children's party arena and marquee wasn't quite

finished but was on its way. They'd called it Noah's Ark and, as well as a wooden ark you could fit thirty kids into, there were all sorts of wooden and plush animals, teddies, rocking horses, wombats and koala bears and Mia's favourites, white unicorns, all two by two.

But through it all she hadn't laid eyes on Carlos.

He'd been as good as his word; he'd been, despite keeping an eye on all her ideas, good to work with, except she hadn't worked with him at all. It had been done entirely at second hand through his secretary, Carol, and a variety of construction staff.

Mia had wondered if she'd be expected to cater for any O'Connor Construction functions but she had not.

Now, though, she was about to be thrown in at the deep end, as she thought of it. She'd been asked to put on the christening party for Juanita's baby.

'Make that babies,' she said faintly to Gail when she put the phone down on Carlos's half-sister. 'She's had twins!'

Gail started to laugh. 'It's all right; I don't suppose they'll have to have twin parties. But tell me what she wants.'

'Well, the actual baptism is to take place in the local church. Then she wants a light luncheon here in the house or garden, depending on the weather. And then, because there'll be quite a few kids, she wants them to go down to Noah's Ark.'

'You've been wanting to give Noah a test run. Now's your chance. How long have we got to prepare for this bash?'

'A month. We don't have to worry about a christening cake—the twins' step-grandfather will make it.'

Gail grinned mischievously. 'I told you it was handy to have a chef in the family.'

'So you did.' Mia rotated her pencil between her fingers and fell silent.

'How about their uncle?' Gail asked after a time.

Mia looked up with her eyebrows raised.

'Carlos?' Gail elucidated somewhat sardonically. 'The guy you got yourself all tied up in knots about, remember?'

'I didn't,' Mia said mechanically.

Gail simply stared at her.

'Oh, all right!' Mia closed her eyes in patent irritation. 'There's no "how about it" at all. I haven't seen or heard from him for months. For all I know, he could have married a...an Eskimo.'

'Now that I very much doubt,' Gail pronounced and stood up. 'He's too tall for an igloo. But it could be best to shore up your defences well and truly.'

Mia stared up at her with her heart suddenly in her eyes. 'How do you do that?' she asked out of a dry throat. 'How do you do that?'

'Tell yourself that, whatever he might like to think, you had good reasons for what *you* did.'

'But...but if you're not sure you did?'

'Mia—' Gail planted her fists on the desk and leant on them '—you've got to go with your gut feeling. And if it tells you things are not right, they're not.' Gail straightened.

'How come you're so wise?' Mia asked with just the glint of a tear in her eye.

Gail shrugged. 'My mum says it's easy to be right about other people's problems. And now I'll leave you to design this christening.'

The weather forecast for the day of the christening was not that good—wet and windy.

Mia grumbled under her breath as she read the details the day before but made the usual decision not to take any chances with sodden food, sodden effects or sodden guests.

She'd already partially decorated the dining room to be on the safe side and decided she needed to finish it off.

Rather than going for pastel pinks and blues, she'd used stronger colours and silver ribbons in bunches. For the rest of it she'd relied on magnificent bunches of flowers.

But some of the ribbons were coming undone and she fetched the ladder and climbed up to retie them.

It was a labour intensive job, getting up and down the ladder and moving it around the room as well as stretching her neck. Which might have been why she came to grief opposite the doorway to the hall.

She must not have had the ladder properly balanced because, as she started to climb down, it wobbled, she lost her footing and, with a startled cry, began to fall.

At first she didn't recognise the pair of arms that caught her. It flashed through her mind that it must be Bill, for once in his life, where she was concerned, anyway, in the right place at the right time.

Then recognition seeped through her pores—Carlos.

'Mia,' he growled, 'you could have broken your back or your head—couldn't you be more careful?'

'Carlos—' she said faintly; he still had her in his arms '—that's funny, isn't it?'

'What's funny?'

'I haven't seen you for months but, once again, it's in an injury situation. Well, no.' She slipped out of his arms. 'I'm fine! Thanks to you. But what are you doing here? The christening isn't until tomorrow,' she said foolishly.

He cast her a frowning look. 'I know that. I came to see you.'

It was her turn to frown. 'Does that mean you're driving back to Sydney, then up again tomorrow?'

He shook his head. 'I'm staying here.'

Mia's mouth fell open.

'Oh, not in your loft,' he drawled, 'but, according to what Gail told Carol, not that Gail knew why Carol was asking, the honeymoon suite is vacant tonight so I thought I'd give it a try. I also thought it was time to have a guided tour of all the changes and improvements.'

'By all means,' Mia heard herself say. 'I was wondering when you would want to see what you'd paid for.'

They stood back and studied each other.

Mia's heart was still beating rapidly beneath the pink blouse she wore with jeans, her cheeks were flushed and her hair was coming loose.

She thought he was taller than she remembered, then realised it was because she was barefoot. She put her hands to her cheeks, then looked around for her shoes.

'I'm sorry I'm so disorganised,' she gabbled, finding herself in complete disarray. 'Actually, I'm not really disorganised. I'm just…' She stopped helplessly and put a hand to her throat. 'Why did you want to see me?'

'We don't need to talk here, do we?' he countered.

Mia licked her lips. 'Where would you like to go?'

'Show me Noah's Ark first.'

'It was only finished a week or so ago,' Mia said as he looked around. 'So I'm really looking forward to giving it a trial run.' She grimaced. 'That doesn't mean to say I'm experimenting with Juanita's guests; it's all safe and sound—I just hope the kids will like it.'

Carlos picked up a wooden giraffe and a smile twisted his lips. 'They will.'

'There are things for older children to do.'

'You've done well, Miss Gardiner.'

She looked up at him. 'Is something wrong?' she asked because he seemed like a stranger to her, because she seemed to be fluttering like a trapped butterfly around him, but there was no light in him, just a very different Carlos O'Connor.

'You could say so.'

'What?' Her eyes were wide and dark and supremely anxious. 'What is it?' She put a trembling hand on his sleeve. 'Tell me.'

He covered her hand with his briefly. 'Just tired, I guess. I only got home from a European trip this morning. OK, now for the much-vaunted honeymoon suite. Lead on.'

Mia hesitated, not entirely convinced he was being honest. 'All right. I'll have to get the keys from the main house, then we can drive your car down.'

Fortunately, Gail had gone into Katoomba on an errand, so as Mia collected the keys she didn't have to attempt any explanations. She did collect a small basket of dairy products, fresh rolls and fruit to take down to the honeymoon suite.

'So,' she said a few minutes later, 'this is it.'

Carlos looked around at the spacious, uncluttered sheer elegance and luxury of the suite, at the stone fireplace and the lovely art on the walls.

Mia moved over to the windows and swept back the curtains and had to smile because the magnificent view down Mount Wilson in the late afternoon sunlight always had that effect on her.

She turned to Carlos. 'It doesn't look like it at the moment, but there's rain predicted for tomorrow. Uh… you'll probably want to have a rest. If you want a snack I brought some fresh rolls, some cheese and other stuff but—' she moved into the galley-style kitchen and opened an iridium fridge '—there should be a gourmet pack here. Yes. Some smoked salmon, anchovies, olives. Uh…beer, wine and champagne as well as spirits.'

She opened another cupboard and revealed a coffee-maker. 'And there's tea and coffee, and here—' She stopped because he walked up to her and took her hand.

'You don't have to sell the place to me, Mia,' he said quietly.

'You did pay for it. And I haven't shown you the bedroom.'

He shrugged. 'Sit down. Glasses?'

Mia hesitated, then pointed to a cupboard.

'Champagne OK with you?' He raised an eyebrow at her.

'Well, one probably won't hurt,' she temporised, then, at the look of irony in his eyes, put her hands to her cheeks as she felt herself blush and, in disarray again, sat down on a stool at the breakfast bar after nearly knocking it over.

He said nothing as he removed the foil from the champagne cork and unwound the wire. It popped discreetly and he poured the bubbly golden liquid into two cut-glass flutes.

'Cheers.' He slid a glass towards her and sat down diagonally opposite her on another stool.

'Cheers!' Mia raised her glass, then took an urgent sip. 'Oh.' She started to slide off the stool. 'I can put together a snack, won't take a moment.'

'Mia, no.'

She stilled.

'Tell me something,' he went on. 'Are you happy?'

She stared at him. 'I...I'm doing fine.'

'Not quite the same thing,' he observed, then gestured, 'except that in your case it might be.'

'What do you mean?'

He looked down at his glass. 'Six months ago I came up here to ask you again to marry me.'

Her lips parted and her eyes were stunned.

'I was going to tell you about Nina—I did, but only part of it,' he went on. 'I was going to suggest we put all the past behind us, not only her but West Windward. I was going to remind you of Byron Bay if you still had reservations.' He stopped and studied her and she shivered for some reason

'Only to discover,' he went on, 'that the one thing that really affected you was the concept of Bellbird being sold. That shocked you to tears and spurred you into making a partnership offer, that's all. That's, incidentally, what made me wonder if "doing fine" in a career and business sense is all that matters to you.'

Mia made a small sound in her throat—a sound of protest.

'Or is it that you still can't forgive me for West Windward, Mia? And my mother? Is that why you could be the way you were at Byron but then all you had to offer me was a business proposition?'

She licked her lips. 'Carlos, did you think all *you* had to do was tell me about Nina and Talbot and I'd fall into your arms? Is that what you're trying to say? I hadn't seen or heard a word from you for *four* months.'

He rubbed his jaw. 'No,' he said at last. 'But I couldn't find the words to tell you that I did try to stop her going off with Talbot. I did try to explain to her what had happened with my father—she was justifiably horrified. She asked me—' he paused, looking tortured '—what I was going to do to wreck *your* life. I don't know if she had any inkling that I'd already damaged it or if it was simply a shot in the dark, but it had a powerful effect on me.'

Mia stared at him, transfixed. 'What do you mean?'

'It made me think maybe my best bet was to avoid you. It made me doubt my judgement, even my sanity. She may never realise it, she may never have intended it as such, but she completely destabilised me with that one little question.'

'So you stayed away?'

'I stayed away—it was also what you wanted,' he reminded her. 'But the day before you were due to leave I knew I couldn't live with myself if I didn't see how you were. But that,' he said with palpable irony, 'led me down the rocky road to hell.'

Mia blinked. 'I was upset to think of Bellbird being sold,' she whispered, 'but I still believed it wasn't over between you and Nina. I couldn't decide what would be worse for you, to see her happy with Talbot or unhappy.'

'No,' he said, 'it is over, it is done with. I'm happy to see her happy, at last.'

Mia closed her eyes. And a surge of something she'd never known before ran through her, a powerful urge to clear her soul of all its secrets.

Her lashes flew up. 'There's one thing you don't understand about me, Carlos. Yes, I may be single-minded in a business sense. Yes, it means a lot to me to succeed because the more I do the fainter the memory of being branded the housekeeper's daughter grows. But it doesn't stop there.'

'What about Byron?' he asked tautly.

'Byron was lovely,' she said with the first sign of

tears in her eyes. 'But you got the shock of your life
that night. So did Nina.' She drained her glass. 'I can't
forget it.'

He made an involuntary movement towards her, then
stilled and poured more champagne.

'Thanks,' she said huskily. 'I told you once I wasn't
going to be used to break Nina's heart. Well, I'll never
know about that but—' she stopped and drew a deep
breath, then trembled as the shutters of her mind fell
away and for the first time she really understood her
own secrets '—you mean far too much to me to s-see
you—' her voice broke '—tied to someone you don't
love deeply.'

'Mia,' he said roughly.

But she held up her hand. 'The other thing is—' She
stopped and sighed and soldiered on. 'The other thing
is…I have an enormous inferiority complex.' Her eyes
were wet and dark. 'I didn't really understand it myself,
but Juanita is so sure of herself, for example. And Nina,
that night. She was so poised—until you told her we
were getting married. Poised and classy. It's not how I
see myself, not around you. It's something that holds
me back without me realising it.'

She rubbed her face. 'So you see, Nina is not the
only one with complexes.'

He stared at her incredulously. 'Say that again?'

'No, Carlos—' she sniffed '—you heard.'

'I may have but it's hard to believe.'

'It shouldn't be, you—'

'I caused it?' he broke in.

'It might just be the way I'm made,' she said miserably.

He studied her for a long moment, her wet spiky lashes, that luscious mouth, her wayward hair, the lovely trim figure, and knew he had to pull out all the stops because he'd made all sorts of mistakes with this woman and it was killing him. Killing him to think Bellbird meant more to her than he did…. But how to right those mistakes? If only he could get her to laugh with him. Maybe the simple truth? It had all the makings of comedy. Well, a farce anyway…

'These have been the hardest six months of my life,' he said.

She looked at him with a faint frown.

'I've fulfilled one of my father's dreams, to have construction sites on the four corners of a major city intersection, to have O'Connor Construction billboards plastered on all four corners.'

'Oh. Congratulations.' But she looked at him uncertainly, not sure what his tone meant or where this was leading.

'Thanks.' He shrugged. 'It didn't help.'

'What do you mean?'

'It didn't help me to view him more affectionately. If anything I was more annoyed than ever. And it's a nightmare scenario, traffic-wise. Then there's my mother.'

Mia's frown grew.

'Yep.' He moved his glass. 'I've always taken her with a grain of salt.' He grimaced. 'What I mean to say is, I've recognised what motivates her, family loyalty above all, and I've dealt with the consequences without too much angst. Except in your case and then it was too late.' He studied his glass and pushed it away, as if it was annoying him too. 'But lately she and her "celebrity" chef husband have been irritating the life out of me. Turns out he's as much of a raving snob as she is, hard as that is to imagine.'

Mia blinked. 'A chef?'

A crooked grin twisted his lips. 'You're as bad as she is, as he is. Yes. He cannot remain silent on any topic relating to food and beverage. He's positively painful on the subject of what wines go with this, that and the other. On what is the correct way to cook this, that and the other, on the best restaurants, not—' he shook his forefinger '—only in Australia but the whole world.'

'Oh, dear.'

He eyed her keenly. 'As you say. Then there's Juanita. As a single half-sister she always had quite a bracing personality but she could be a lot of fun. As a married matron and mother of twins she's insufferably smug, another snob and—' He broke off and gestured. 'I don't know how Damien puts up with her.'

Mia put her hands on the island bench. 'Carlos—'

But he waved her to silence. 'Hang on. Then there's the construction industry in general. Now, I may have had issues with my father but I'm actually a passionate engineer and builder—or I was.' He looked supremely sombre.

'Not anymore?' Mia hazarded.

'I couldn't give a damn if I never built another thing.'

'Carlos—' she paused '—I'm not a hundred per cent sure you're serious.'

'I am, and there's more. I've lived like a monk ever since Byron Bay because I haven't been able to have you, Mia.'

Mia took an unexpected breath.

He waited a moment, then he slid his hand across the island bench and touched her fingers with his.

For a moment she was frozen, hardly even breathing, her eyes huge.

'Really?' she said at last.

He nodded.

'You...you tried?'

He nodded again. 'A couple of times. With disastrous consequences. How about you?'

'Oh, I didn't want to so I didn't even think of trying,' she assured him, then she broke off and bit her lip.

The pressure of his fingers increased on hers. 'Do you think that means...anything?'

'Carlos...' She took a breath.

'Mia, I can't live without you,' he said. 'It's killing me. All the mistakes I made are killing me. As for your complexes—' he closed his eyes briefly '—please throw them away because they mean nothing to me. And please take me on—you can redecorate me, renegotiate me but if you don't restore me I'm in serious trouble. And that's the plain, unvarnished truth.'

Her lips trembled and, hard as she tried, she couldn't stop herself from starting to smile.

Carlos got up cautiously and came round the island

bench. He stopped in front of Mia and tilted her chin up gently. And there was a question in his eyes.

'Oh, look,' Mia whispered. 'I'm not sure why, but I think I've always loved you, Carlos, and I always will.'

'Is there anything wrong with that?' he queried.

'No. Not anymore. I don't seem to have any fight left in me,' she conceded. 'I've missed you so much.'

He pulled her into his arms. 'Same here. More than you could ever know. Mia—will you marry me?'

'Yes. Yes, I will,' she said and found she couldn't stop smiling.

'They're back, your dimples,' he said unsteadily.

'That can only be because you're back,' she told him.

'Thanks for that.' And he started to kiss her.

Quite some time later they stirred in each other's arms. They'd moved from the island bench to a settee in the lounge area, one that overlooked the view—a view that was dominated by some magnificent purple thunderheads.

'I told you rain was forecast,' she said as she nuzzled into his shoulder.

He stroked her hair. 'Juanita will be upset—upset that she can't control the weather.'

Mia gave a spurt of laughter although she said, 'Now that's unkind. She's not that bossy. Is she?'

He shrugged and traced the line of her jaw with his finger. 'She has actually run into one spot of bother with Damien. Over naming the twins.'

'Oh, tell me about it, and about them! All I know is that it's a boy and a girl.'

His fingers traced a path down her neck to the little hollows at the base of her throat. 'True. And Juanita wants to name them Charlotte and Henry—if that isn't aspiring to the aristocracy I don't know what is. But Damien wants to call them Barbara and Banjo. His grandmother who he's very fond of is a Barbara—I don't know where he got Banjo from—apart from Banjo Paterson. Up until I last saw them yesterday, the issue was still to be decided.'

Mia had to laugh. 'They're leaving it a bit late.'

'Mmm,' he said, sounding preoccupied and his fingers slid down to the top button of her blouse. 'I'm a godfather, by the way. You'll probably have to help me out a bit there.'

But Mia had other things on her mind as he flicked open the button, and then the next and the next and slipped his hands around her back and released her bra.

She took several ragged breaths but didn't protest as he drew her blouse off and then helped her out of her bra.

Nor did she protest when he said, 'What we need is a bed.'

'This might be a good place to remedy that.' Her dimples appeared. 'You ain't seen nothing yet, Mr O'Connor,' she teased. 'Not until you see the bedroom.'

'OK, lead on.' He picked her up.

What he said next was somewhat different.

'Holy…mackerel!' He looked around the honeymoon suite bedroom, a symphony of white and green with a huge bed piled with cushions, an exquisite original painting of flowers taking up almost all of one wall, deep pile carpet, a padded velvet headboard and a beautiful crystal chandelier.

Mia laughed softly. 'Think I might have gone overboard?'

'Not at all.' He put her down on the bed and together they tossed aside all the silken cushions, then they shed their clothes and Mia could not doubt his desperate hunger for her, nor hers for him.

And when they crashed back to earth, he held her and helped her down from the heights in such a way that caused her to say with real gratitude, 'You make me feel as if I've come home.'

He cradled her to him. 'You make me feel the same. When will you marry me?'

'Whenever we can.'

He rubbed his jaw. 'I've got this damn christening tomorrow. I don't suppose I can get out of that.'

'Oh, no, you shouldn't! Anyway, we couldn't do it tomorrow, could we?'

He leant up on his elbow. 'No. I don't know how long it takes.' He tidied some damp wayward strands of her hair and pulled a silk coverlet over them. 'Will you come to the christening with me?'

'Carlos, I'll be working at it,' she reminded him.

'No,' he replied firmly. 'Get Gail and her mother and anyone else you can raise—Bill and Lucy—you've done it before. I need you with me, otherwise my family might prompt me into…being rude or unkind to them.'

Mia giggled but she soon sobered. 'Your mother will

be livid. Perhaps an occasion like a christening isn't the right time to break the news to her.'

'My mother is not nearly as interfering as she was, Mia, but, whatever, there's no point in hiding it.'

Mia thought for a moment, then, 'No. Anyway, I think we have to break the news to Gail. She'll be wondering where on earth I've got to.'

He stretched and looked disinclined to move.

'She could even come looking for me,' Mia said gravely, 'and we didn't lock the door.'

Carlos swore beneath his breath, then rolled over and enveloped her in a bear hug. 'All right. I get the message. I don't suppose we could shower together?'

'Ah.' Mia looked mischievous. 'We sure can. Come and have a look. This is the bathroom to beat all bathrooms.'

'There you are, Mia!' Gail said as Mia walked into her office to find Gail behind the desk fielding the phone. 'I've been looking for you. There's—oh, no,' she added as Carlos walked in behind Mia. 'Not you again.'

Carlos looked briefly startled, then amused. 'Sorry, Gail. I didn't realise I was on your blacklist. Why am I?'

Mia cleared her throat and started to speak but Gail overrode her. 'Why are you? You come and you go, Mr O'Connor, and every time you go I'm left to pick up the pieces.'

'*Gail*!' Mia protested.

Gail swung towards her. 'It's true. You've been devastated every time it's happened and—'

'Gail—' it was Carlos who intervened and he took

Mia's hand '—there won't be any more of that. Mia's agreed to marry me, we're very much in love and we've smoothed out all our problems. But I'd just like to say I can't thank you enough for being such a good friend to Mia.'

Gail stood stock-still then she ran round the desk to embrace Mia and then Carlos

'Oh, I'm so happy,' she cried tearfully. 'I don't know if I'm coming or going. When? When's the wedding? Are you having it up here? You could leave it all to me, you know.'

Mia was also mopping up some tears as she said, 'We haven't made any plans yet but, Gail, you'll have to handle the christening tomorrow because I'm going as a guest.'

'With pleasure.' Gail struck a nonchalant pose. 'I could do it in my sleep.'

Mia and Carlos were still chuckling as they walked into the garden as the sun set but he stopped suddenly and put his arms around her.

'I feel terrible,' he said, looking down at her.

'Why?'

'For leaving you devastated up here. I'm not sure why you've forgiven me.'

She slipped her arms around his neck. 'What Gail doesn't realise is that I sent you away.' She stood on her toes and kissed him.

'Even if it devastated you?'

She nodded and laid her head on his shoulder. 'What about you?'

'Angry, incredulous, bloody-minded probably says it well, every time I drove down this blasted mountain. Sick to think it meant more to you than I did, this place. All in all, a mess.'

'Well—' Mia stirred '—since it seems we've both been to hell and back, let's go to heaven.'

He lifted his head, his grey eyes amused. 'I hope you don't mean that literally?'

'Depends! Let's go back to the honeymoon suite—'

'You're not worried about putting the cart before the horse?' he broke in gravely.

'Not in the least. I was thinking of cooking you dinner, you see—an inch-thick steak, chips that are crisp on the outside and fluffy inside—oh, some English mustard hot enough to make your eyes water, some salad, but only iceberg lettuce, of course, maybe some mushrooms. I just have to collect the ingredients from the house.'

'Now that,' he drawled, 'is an offer I can't refuse.'

'Good.' She dimpled. 'Then we can worry about putting the cart before the horse.'

He grinned down at her. 'I can see you're going to be a right handful, Miss Gardiner.'

'It's my aim,' she said pertly.

CHAPTER TEN

THE DAY JUANITA'S twins were christened was a day to remember. It was cool and showery, as predicted.

Mia drove to her cottage and collected her clothes.

As she was about to climb back into the car, Bill intercepted her with a particularly Bill James-like salutation. He was driving the property utility, laden with bags of fertiliser, and he drew up beside her and leant out of his window.

'Hi, Mia! Heard the news, by the way—you'll be much happier as a married woman, believe me.'

Mia drew a deep breath and cautioned herself not to lose her temper. 'Thank you, Bill. I...I will try to be.'

'And you give Carlos my best wishes. I guess he must know what he's getting into, although not many of us guys do!' And, laughing cheerfully, he drove on.

Mia contemplated kicking something but refrained.

She must have still been wearing the remnants of a militant expression when she arrived back at the honeymoon suite, however, because Carlos immediately said to her, 'What's wrong?'

'Nothing.' She put down her clothes. 'How do you know anything's wrong, anyway?

'You look—' he meditated '—as if you'd like to kick the cat.'

Mia grimaced, then had to laugh ruefully and she told him about Bill.

'Of course I wouldn't dare to agree with him,' he replied with utter false gravity.

Mia clicked her tongue. 'You men are all the same.' She paused and fiddled with her cosmetic purse before putting it down beside her clothes and starting to plait her fingers.

'Carlos, I'm nervous. I'm really nervous. I don't think I can do this.'

'Mia—' he linked his arms around her waist '—yes, you can. Anyway, they all know now.'

She put her hands on his chest, her eyes wide. 'Your mother? Did she have a fit?'

'No. She told me it was about time I settled down. Juanita said the same. Mind you—' he frowned faintly '—I got the feeling something else was going on. They both seemed preoccupied, if not to say tense, and that was before I broke our news.'

Mia relaxed a bit. 'I hope so. I mean…all I mean is I'd rather not be the headline news.'

He bent his head and kissed her. 'You were my headline news last night. You have a unique way of putting the cart before the horse.'

A tingle ran through Mia at the memory of their night. 'It was lovely, wasn't it?' she said softly.

This time he hugged her, then, with an obvious effort, put her away from him. 'Maybe we should get dressed,' he suggested. 'We have been known to—' there was a wicked little glint in his grey eyes '—get carried away when we should be on our way out.'

Mia laughed and stood on her toes and kissed him. 'I remember. I'm going.'

He groaned but didn't try to stop her.

Mia changed into a figure-hugging yellow dress and a smoky grey-blue jacket belted at the waist. She'd decided not to wear any kind of hat for this christening and saw no reason to change her mind now she was a guest so she left her hair wild and riotous, just as he liked it.

But she drew an unexpected breath at the sight of Carlos in a pinstriped charcoal suit, pale green shirt and darker green tie.

'You look seriously handsome,' she told him.

He came to stand right in front of her. 'Good enough to be a godfather?'

'Oh, definitely!'

'Well, you look gorgeous, Mia, darling.' He took her hand. 'Ready?'

She hesitated, then nodded. 'Ready,' she said quietly.

It stopped raining as the baptism proceeded.

There was even some sunlight bringing rays of colour into the church through the stained glass windows, violet and topaz, jade and ruby.

Arancha was arrayed in ivory shantung: an exqui-
sitely tailored suit and a poppy-pink hat. She had acknowledged Mia with an almost non-existent kiss on
the cheek but she'd said, 'Let's be friends, Mia, let's
be friends.'

And Mia, who had searched her heart and known
she could never altogether forgive Arancha, had contrived to reply warmly, for Carlos's sake, 'Yes, let's.'

She'd then been introduced to Arancha's celebrity
chef, who'd told her he could probably give her some
pretty good tips on cuisine and all sorts of things to do
with the catering business.

Mia had felt Carlos tense beside her so she'd smiled
brilliantly and replied that she'd love to hear them.

Juanita wore violet linen and Damien wore a dark
suit. They both looked a little shell-shocked for some
reason and each carried a sleeping baby garbed in a
sumptuous lacy gown.

It wasn't until the naming of the babies came about
that most of the mysteries of the morning were explained. The girl was baptised Alegria Arancha and
the boy Benito Francis.

'Good Spanish names,' Arancha said quite audibly,
'and why not include the mother's mother?'

Mia heard Carlos suck in a breath but it wasn't until
the baptism was over and they were in the car head-
ing back to Bellbird that they were able to give way to
their mirth.

'For crying out loud,' Carlos said. 'She must have

bulldozed away at both of them to get them to change their minds.'

'I thought you told me she didn't interfere anymore?' Mia had to dab carefully at her eyes so as not to smudge her mascara.

'I didn't think she did! Something about Charlotte or Barbara, Henry or Banjo must have really riled her.'

'Well, I thought Juanita could stand up to her.'

'I thought she could. I was wrong. Mind you, the fight over names between Juanita and Damien was beginning to assume epic proportions so it could even have been a stroke of genius.'

Mia put her hanky away but she was still chuckling.

'You were good with my mother and her chef,' Carlos said as he swung into Bellbird's drive.

'I intend to stay good with her.' Mia put a hand on his arm. 'I don't know why but I feel different all of a sudden.'

'Different?' He looked comically apprehensive for a moment. 'How so?'

Mia drew a deep breath. 'I don't feel like the housekeeper's daughter any more. I wonder why?'

'Could it be because you're about to become—and willingly—the padrone's wife?' he suggested.

But Mia shook her head although she acknowledged his rueful look with the glint of a smile. 'No, I think it's because suddenly you all seem so normal.'

'I would have thought we were all bordering on insanity,' he objected and pulled up in front of the house.

'Not really. You have your fights, your ups and downs, your loyalties, your crazy times, just like everyone else. Look—' she shook her head and her expression was wry '—I know it sounds ridiculous to you for me to say I hadn't seen you all like that before, but it's true. And it makes me feel different.'

He turned to her and put an arm along the back of her seat. 'Are you serious?'

'Uh-huh!'

'Well—' he paused '—I've had a thought. It's occurred to me that I've neglected them for a time. It's occurred to me I ought to undertake some fence-mending exercises, like somehow getting Damien to forgive my mother for insisting he call his son Benito. Ditto Juanita. And it looked to me as if Damien and Juanita are feeling just about as hostile towards each other as it's possible to be, wouldn't you agree?'

'Oh, I do! They didn't even look at each other.'

'Right. I must say, I don't know what I can do about the celebrity chef who's popped up in our midst but—do you remember the wedding you had here that was about to flop unless you were able to pull something out of the hat?'

Mia's eyes widened. 'Yes...'

'From memory, you actually exhorted me to make the kind of speech only I could make to liven things up or you'd scream blue murder?'

Mia's lips twitched. 'I do,' she said solemnly.

'Can you promise me, though, that if I do stop this christening from flopping and manage to turn it into a happy, even joyful occasion, you won't go back to feeling like the housekeeper's daughter?'

'I won't, I promise,' she said huskily. 'Please do it. I love you,' she told him, smiling through the tears in her eyes. 'I love you, Carlos O'Connor.'

* * * * *

ROMANCE

His Most Exquisite Conquest	Emma Darcy
One Night Heir	Lucy Monroe
His Brand of Passion	Kate Hewitt
The Return of Her Past	Lindsay Armstrong
The Couple who Fooled the World	Maisey Yates
Proof of Their Sin	Dani Collins
In Petrakis's Power	Maggie Cox
A Shadow of Guilt	Abby Green
Once is Never Enough	Mira Lyn Kelly
The Unexpected Wedding Guest	Aimee Carson
A Cowboy To Come Home To	Donna Alward
How to Melt a Frozen Heart	Cara Colter
The Cattleman's Ready-Made Family	Michelle Douglas
Rancher to the Rescue	Jennifer Faye
What the Paparazzi Didn't See	Nicola Marsh
My Boyfriend and Other Enemies	Nikki Logan
The Gift of a Child	Sue MacKay
How to Resist a Heartbreaker	Louisa George

MEDICAL

Dr Dark and Far-Too Delicious	Carol Marinelli
Secrets of a Career Girl	Carol Marinelli
A Date with the Ice Princess	Kate Hardy
The Rebel Who Loved Her	Jennifer Taylor

Mills & Boon® Large Print
July 2013

ROMANCE

Playing the Dutiful Wife	Carol Marinelli
The Fallen Greek Bride	Jane Porter
A Scandal, a Secret, a Baby	Sharon Kendrick
The Notorious Gabriel Diaz	Cathy Williams
A Reputation For Revenge	Jennie Lucas
Captive in the Spotlight	Annie West
Taming the Last Acosta	Susan Stephens
Guardian to the Heiress	Margaret Way
Little Cowgirl on His Doorstep	Donna Alward
Mission: Soldier to Daddy	Soraya Lane
Winning Back His Wife	Melissa McClone

HISTORICAL

The Accidental Prince	Michelle Willingham
The Rake to Ruin Her	Julia Justiss
The Outrageous Belle Marchmain	Lucy Ashford
Taken by the Border Rebel	Blythe Gifford
Unmasking Miss Lacey	Isabelle Goddard

MEDICAL

The Surgeon's Doorstep Baby	Marion Lennox
Dare She Dream of Forever?	Lucy Clark
Craving Her Soldier's Touch	Wendy S. Marcus
Secrets of a Shy Socialite	Wendy S. Marcus
Breaking the Playboy's Rules	Emily Forbes
Hot-Shot Doc Comes to Town	Susan Carlisle

GEN STD LP

Mills & Boon® Hardback
August 2013

ROMANCE

MEDICAL

ROMANCE

Master of her Virtue	Miranda Lee
The Cost of her Innocence	Jacqueline Baird
A Taste of the Forbidden	Carole Mortimer
Count Valieri's Prisoner	Sara Craven
The Merciless Travis Wilde	Sandra Marton
A Game with One Winner	Lynn Raye Harris
Heir to a Desert Legacy	Maisey Yates
Sparks Fly with the Billionaire	Marion Lennox
A Daddy for Her Sons	Raye Morgan
Along Came Twins…	Rebecca Winters
An Accidental Family	Ami Weaver

HISTORICAL

The Dissolute Duke	Sophia James
His Unusual Governess	Anne Herries
An Ideal Husband?	Michelle Styles
At the Highlander's Mercy	Terri Brisbin
The Rake to Redeem Her	Julia Justiss

MEDICAL

The Brooding Doc's Redemption	Kate Hardy
An Inescapable Temptation	Scarlet Wilson
Revealing The Real Dr Robinson	Dianne Drake
The Rebel and Miss Jones	Annie Claydon
The Son that Changed his Life	Jennifer Taylor
Swallowbrook's Wedding of the Year	Abigail Gordon

GEN STD LP

Mills & Boon® Online

Discover more romance at
www.millsandboon.co.uk

- **FREE** online reads
- **Books** up to one month before shops
- **Browse our books** before you buy

...and much more!

For exclusive competitions and instant updates:

 Like us on **facebook.com/millsandboon**

 Follow us on **twitter.com/millsandboon**

 Join us on **community.millsandboon.co.uk**

Visit us Online Sign up for our FREE eNewsletter at **www.millsandboon.co.uk**

WEB/M&B/RTL5/HB